JAC

Jack walked back into the bedroom and looked into his old school trunk where he'd laid his baby after her feed. She was wrapped snugly up in towels and was gurgling happily. He looked into her eyes and smiled.

If he was actually going to be a father then he was going to have to get himself organised. He called a taxi. Then he picked her out of the suitcase and held her up to his face. There was something absolutely irresistible about her. Her eyes sparkled and she made him feel light-headed. She made him want to protect her.

'So, they've all ganged up on Daddy. Well, that's fine. This isn't so difficult after all, is it?' He held her close so that their noses touched. He giggled. 'It's a piece of piss!'

JACK AND SARAH
based on a film by Tim Sullivan

JAMES MAW

Mandarin

A Mandarin Paperback

JACK AND SARAH

First published in Great Britain 1995
by Mandarin Paperbacks
an imprint of Reed Books Ltd
Michelin House, 81 Fulham Road, London SW3 6RB
and Auckland, Melbourne, Singapore and Toronto

Copyright © James Maw 1995
based on an original screenplay by Tim Sullivan

A CIP catalogue record for this title
is available from the British Library
ISBN 0 7493 3620 X

Typeset by Deltatype Limited, Ellesmere Port, Cheshire
Printed and bound in Great Britain
by Cox & Wyman Ltd, Reading

For Rachel

1

'That's a substantial sum of money, again, sir!' said the young woman behind the bullet-proof glass. Jack narrowed his eyes. Yes, it was, it was a lot of money again, to take out in cash.

He could see she was dying to ask what he did with it all. But he didn't have time for this, not this afternoon and he wanted to leap over the counter top, way over the glass shield, and count out the fifty-pound notes himself. Jack looked at his watch.

'Would you excuse me?' she said, and began scrolling through the interminable roll-call of his deposit account. A continuous record lately of extravagant withdrawals.

He looked toward the window. Through the roped-off line of shop assistants with cash boxes and businessmen chained to attaché cases, he could see his car across the street. It was parked at a precarious angle, and looked as if it had stopped very suddenly indeed. It was beside a parking meter with the penalty flag joyfully flying. Damn, he was going to be very late.

The young woman looked up and smiled. He attempted his most winning smile in return, in the hope of speeding things up. It was the smile he'd used as a schoolboy whenever he'd been up to no good. When he'd been called into the housemaster's study. Generally to explain some misdemeanour, like the time he was

1

accused of affixing a rather phallic appendage to the founder's statue. On Parents' Day. It had worked then, and on various occasions since. It worked with Sarah, his wife, most of the time. It worked at the law firm where he was a partner. And he hoped now that it would suffice for a man who'd just performed a certain amount of abuse on a parking meter.

The teller began counting the fifty notes. A hundred of them, some new, some old, and some which the recession seemed to have hit particularly hard. He looked furiously up at the ceiling. My God, they were fast enough when they wanted money from him. Why didn't it work the other way round as well? He began thinking about where he could lay his hands on a sawn- off shotgun . . .

At the same time, on the other side of London, Jack's wife Sarah was lying on a bed. It was a small room with pale-blue soothing hospital walls. The radiographer spread a cold, translucent gel across her belly and began to glide an electronic sensor slowly across her white skin.

Where was Jack? thought Sarah. Something really foolish must have happened to him. This was their first baby and Jack had never been more full of anything in his life. He loved going along to her scans. He loved it so much, in fact, that she was almost entirely ignored during the whole process. Jack asked so many questions of the radiographer, and frequently had his face right up against the screen so that no one else could see very much at all. Then he'd turn to Sarah, and kiss her.

'There you are, look,' said the radiographer. 'There's the baby's feet, and you can just work out the toes there. There's the nose, you see?'

Sarah smiled.

Every time she came for a scan the miracle of it seemed ever more delightful and amazing. She looked deep into the screen. Even though the pictures looked as if they were being beamed from outer space, it seemed wonderful to her to feel the proximity of their child's birth in this way. Even the radiographer's eyes were bright with it, though she must see this a dozen times every day, she didn't seem to have lost the wonder of it either.

'Oh look there,' she said, 'there's the baby yawning.' It seemed the oddest, but most beautiful thing to see on a screen. A young life yawning in the warm water of her womb. At ease inside her, peaceful, and perfect, taking a late-afternoon nap. She almost cried with happiness. They would do everything for this child, everything . . .

Back in the bank, the teller had stopped counting midway through the wodge and shook her head.

'Look at this note here,' she said. She held it up to show him. Shaking her head in professional disdain. Someone had scribbled in blue Biro across the face of the note. What sort of people use denominations such as this as notepaper?

Jack was almost beside himself. What the hell did it matter if someone had scrawled a phone number on it? He was still perfectly capable of spending it. He would have missed a whole scan.

Ordinarily he prided himself in being something of an entertainment in the bank. Or in the supermarket, or sharing a cab with a stranger. Only yesterday he'd intervened as negotiator, during a multiple trolley mix-up in Waitrose. Sarah, who had remained in the car, had heard the laughter from the parking lot, as he ran a commentary on the contents of their trolleys. As he walked towards her he'd tried to look so innocent that she knew he'd been the cause of the laughter and the scene.

If Sarah left him unattended in a public place for any more than ten minutes there was generally some sort of incident. It could be exhausting, especially when she felt she was breaking all known records for having the longest pregnancy in history.

Jack was an excitable chap, and never more so than now. But, amazing though it was, people still liked him. Even when all he could talk about was the baby. Strangers took to him instantly. People liked to spend time in his company. Even when he was drunk people listened to him, and encouraged him to get worse. He liked to be goaded, he liked people to demand a reaction from him. And they got one.

Sarah looked again at the baby's gently wriggling features on the ultrascan screen. She smiled broadly. One thing was sure, she knew, Jack would make a wonderful father. The next years were going to be fun. She thought of Jack's own father. Jack'd vowed that he was not going to make the mistakes he had. He'd been a distant figure throughout his childhood. Jack said he always seemed to have to search for his name when he returned from some conference or other. She felt sorry for him sometimes. Her own father had died when she was very young, but she had wonderful memories of him.

Although they regularly saw Jack's father, the relationship between them was so cold that it barely existed at all.

Jack was determined, he said, almost every day now, that this baby was going to be loved. Theirs was going to be a House Of Love.

In the bank Jack was now so irritated that he'd developed a fearsome nervous twitch. He hated missing the scan so much, and at this rate he was going to miss the pre-natal class as well. He still had the builders, working on their new house, to pay. He was determined that the bank wasn't going to rob him of his most looked-forward-to social event of the week. If he missed a class, he might never catch up, he'd lose a whole slice of fatherhood, for ever.

The bank teller looked up at him and smiled. She'd found another fifty pound note with a phone number scrawled on it.

'Sometimes,' she said, 'I'm almost tempted to phone them up!' Why the hell had he lumped for the damned chatty one of the Finsbury Circus branch? thought Jack. Why couldn't he have the boring old codger with the Brylcreamed hair?

Finally, with the bulging wodge, all five thousand pounds of it, in his breast pocket, he headed across the bank's concourse towards the door. He could see the appalling course of the afternoon mapped out before him. Now, in a shabby little episode, he'd be deftly mugged in the street. He skidded across the traffic to his car, one hand on his car keys, the other on his breast pocket.

Then he yelled out loud, 'I don't believe it!' as he took

in the offensive notice pasted to his windscreen.

There on the front wheel was a bright yellow clamp. He looked into the eyes of the parking meter with fury. This was institutionalised mugging. It looked so smug in its triumph that he expected another flag to pop up, saying, 'And your car needs a damn good wash too.' It did, the bonnet had a thick film of building-site dust. Jack looked around him in anger. Why had they ever decided to buy a house that basically needed building again from the bottom up?

Then he saw the clamping van. There was still a chance, it had been halted by the traffic lights. Oh, yes? thought Jack. I'm not done for yet. Brace yourself, chum.

He tore back across the road towards it.

Inside, at the wheel, a podgy-faced man with a stupid grin on his face sat listening to his Walkman.

Jack tapped on the window. Then he beat on the window.

'Please, please, excuse me, but it's an emergency!' he called. Of course, he felt like being a great deal more abusive than this right now, but first, he'd try reasonable negotiation. Then he would try an all-out attack on the van.

The passenger door was locked, but there was a tiny gap at the top of the window. Jack jumped up and grabbed on to the door handle with one hand, and the window gap with the other.

But as if all the traffic devices in London were conspiring against him so the traffic lights turned to green. Jack was suddenly propelled into the full traffic flow of Finsbury Circus as he gripped on to the clamping van. The driver remained wilfully oblivious to him.

Jack turned his head sideways and managed to get his mouth into the gap at the top of the window.

'Please, you've got to listen to me, I really am in the most terrible hurry ... I put money in the meter, honestly, you've got to believe me ...' The van swerved across the lanes of traffic with the recklessness of a vehicle above the law, as Jack's legs flailed around him. How much longer could this stupid man possibly think he could ignore him?

As the clamping van tore through Bishopsgate Jack began screaming louder. 'OK, OK, is it money you want? You want money? Right, I'll give you money.' His eyes were wide and glaring.

He began feeding fifty-pound notes through the gap in the window. His knees were now battered and his knuckles sore.

'For God's sake just take the bloody money, take the bloody money!' he yelled.

As a master-builder Nathaniel had enjoyed himself this afternoon at Jack and Sarah's new house in Islington. A new bag of plaster had arrived, and it still sat there, sedately, in the hallway.

It was a pleasant late-January day, with such a quality of clear crisp light, falling on every alcove and cornice of the house, that to build, and disrupt the air with the sound of drills and hammers, would be an affront to nature itself. Added to this, the card game was going particularly well. Rarely was a collection of men, ordinarily engaged with the business of mortar, and grouting, and re-pointing, so blessed with the touch of luck and grace as they were this afternoon. To smash, for a moment, the magical spell of men engaged in the peaceful pursuit of a successful game of chance would be a crime against mankind. So what if their gaming table was an upturned cement-encrusted bucket? These men were the noble heirs to those unsung labourers who had built the Acropolis. And in the background there was the sport of kings, relayed from Cheltenham on the radio, providing a sophisticated air of enchantment for those of the merry band who had ventured to invest in the outcome of the four-thirty. The only sour note of discord in this Elysian bliss was the meagre capacity of the porcelain mugs from which they supped their tea and the occasional absence of handles, caused by the rush with which they had eagerly returned to work on the sudden arrival of their paying host.

It has to be said, that as a master-builder, Nathaniel was a thoughtful man. He had the capacity to consider a project thoroughly, before any action involving actual bricks or mortar was undertaken that might, in the course of time, be detrimental to the overall effect of eventual magnificence.

A car screeched to a halt in the street outside.

'Oh, bugger,' thought Nathaniel as his watchman, drinking tea on the roof, let out a whistle. 'It's him.'

Instantly the cards went into the bucket. The radio was suddenly deafened by the sound of drills. Great planks of wood began their transit around the shell of the house, and the gentle lick of fresh-mixed plaster began its course across a short stretch of the hall wall. Nathaniel had an impressive set of architects' drawings in his hands.

Jack stood for a moment, regaining his breath and calming himself. The man in the clamping van had finally given in to corruption, and it had cost Jack two hundred pounds.

Jack stood in the street for a moment and looked up at the other houses in the square. Fine London townhouses, solid and dignified like Edwardian wedding cakes.

Though sombre clouds were threatening rain, bands of bright warm light fell on the white-painted plasterwork. This would be a good square to live in. There was a little park at the centre of it surrounded by delicately ornate railings. An excellent place for them to play with their baby. Not only was the square itself full of character, it had real characters living there too. Delightfully eccentric elderly ladies who lived in the basement garden flats, throwing clay pots and painting outrageous nudes in oils. There was the editor of a national newspaper just two doors along, and young people, like themselves, lawyers and designers and columnists.

The interiors of the houses were lined with books, fine plants and paintings. The residents held communal barbecues. Their living-rooms glowed in the dusk, into the peaceful, dignified square. All right, it had cost them nearly every penny they had, and as the birth grew nearer, so the renovation work seemed to be getting further away. But at the pub on the corner you could order pigeon for lunch. It would be home.

Perhaps one last push from Nathaniel would do it, and they could settle down to their brave new lives.

Jack looked up at the house they'd bought. At the moment, because of the mass of scaffolding, tarpaulin, buckets dangling from ropes, and a huge orange plastic chute, it did look something like the Pompidou Centre. Or London after the blitz. But when it was done, it would be perfect. When it was done.

Now that he'd got his breath back, and regained his composure, Jack dashed up the steps and into the hallway. Ready for the next battle of the day.

'Hello, there, Reg. I see the plastering's coming on,' he said, over-hopefully, to one of Nathaniel's men.

'Coming on nicely, Jack, very nicely.'

Jack smiled encouragingly. He wanted the builders to like him, even though, he suspected, they must think that he was just a jumped-up young twerp with more money than sense.

They were way behind schedule because Nathaniel had unearthed so many strange structural difficulties with the house. Sometimes when they discussed the slow progress with a simple strip of skirting board they may as well have been organising the raising of the *Mary Rose*. It was news to Jack as well that the entire square had been originally built in the wrong place, and on a tilt, possibly on a Druid ley line, which naturally affected everything. While not actually believing a word of it, and being infuriated by the amount of bullshit he had to take from this man, Nathaniel's conversation was so sparse, that Jack found himself constantly forced to nod in agreement at any titbits he threw him. Before flying into a rage later.

At times his builder could be a master of the one-liner.

'Well it's your rot, isn't it?' was a constant comment of his, and something of an accusation which seemed to be levelled at Jack personally. 'If only your frontage was south-facing,' was another gross error on Jack's part. But the rot, Jack knew, was entirely Nathaniel's.

He asked the plasterer where he could find him, or 'The Boss', as he seemed to have recently got himself trapped into calling him. Nathaniel was on the roof.

Jack took the stairs two at a time. Not because he was so keen to see his builder, but because almost every other stair was still stacked in a great pile in the dining-room. As he turned around the first landing there was a shout of 'Watch the electrics,' from below. In the last twenty-four hours the walls had sprouted even more ancient wiring. The second and third floors were in almost total darkness. Where the lower floors were electrically lethal, so here there was no power at all. Jack negotiated the gaps in the floorboards. As he approached the roof the house seemed to have disintegrated entirely. Reduced to bare joists and ladders.

Jack climbed the ladder and poked his head up into the sky. Nathaniel looked at him, stared back at his architects' drawings for a moment, and laid them aside. Jack clambered to the top of the ladder. He looked at Nathaniel in a nervous state of shock.

'Where's the roof? What's happened to the roof?'

Nathaniel merely nodded towards the chute and the skip in the street below.

'But what if it rains?'

'It won't.'

Nathaniel felt that the less said about it the better. One didn't engage with the client in debates over strategy. Nathaniel referred to this in his own mind as 'damage limitation'. A rather apt phrase in Jack's case, really, thought Nathaniel. How could a punter appreciate that they'd spent the better part of the morning removing it? At one point they'd even run the danger of their labours eating into elevenses. Not only this, but constructing a new roof, from scratch, was an entirely different proposition from merely removing an old one. A roof that had patently been created by Edwardian cowboys. It was a miracle that the slates had not already descended to the street below, slicing off the heads of innocent women and children. Which would invariably involve Jack in even more expense.

Jack muttered, and shook his head. The feeling of exasperation was returning. He reached into his breast pocket and pulled out the bundle of notes.

'It's two hundred short, I'm afraid...' he said. Nathaniel snorted, saw the glare in Jack's eyes, but thought better of saying any more about it. Money, of course, was the one subject Nathaniel was usually prepared to get into lengthy debates about.

The one working telephone in the house began to ring on the ground floor.

'I'd better get that,' said Jack. Nathaniel thrust the four thousand eight hundred pounds into his back pocket, calculating in his mind how much those old roof tiles would probably fetch. He smiled inwardly to himself.

'Right, well, thanks,' said Jack. 'Keep up the good work. Bye.'

Jack answered the telephone. Sarah didn't really appear to believe the tale of the clamping episode, and thought he was probably covering up a much more ridiculous incident. He hadn't mentioned he'd been hanging off the van door, of course. It was just a shame, that's all, she said, that he'd missed another scan. She knew how disappointed he must be, but she couldn't help adding that he'd really have to be a lot more reliable when the baby was born.

She was already at the pre-natal class, which was about to begin, and she suggested that his arse was got over there double-quick if he didn't want to miss all the fun and excitement.

'Of course, darling, of course. Of course. I'm on my way to you now, right away . . .'

He dashed back to his car.

2

The class had already begun when Jack arrived. Couples sat around in a circle earnestly hanging on to every word that the instructor said.

The classes were held in a small, slightly disorganised room on the ground floor of an old building, of definitely faded municipal grandeur, in Islington. They'd chosen a class in Islington because it was near to their new house and it would give them the opportunity to meet people from their new neighbourhood in the same situation as themselves. Now, having met these people, it had most definitely been a rash decision. Relationships formed in pre-natal classes are thankfully not for life, Jack was beginning to realise. As an introduction to new aquaintances, the communal miming of contractions is perhaps not the best footing to get off on. However much fun it is personally.

Other couples in the group were already having coffee with each other and exchanging baby books. Jack, however, had been marked down right from the start as the aloof member of the group. Even so, it still irritated him that he didn't come across as well here as he did in other situations. But then, he told himself, there's very little scope for mischief in a set-up such as this, and they all seemed to be a bit nervous of him. He could sometimes get a little carried away by enthusiasm.

As Jack walked in, they were sitting in pairs, on plastic chairs, practising their breathing. An exercise that he had never really considered necessary, but now it was a major part of his life. He'd really like to master the breathing tonight. You need goals.

He slipped into the empty chair next to Sarah.

'Sorry,' he whispered. He flashed her one of his smiles and she smiled in return and slid her hand, momentarily, into his.

She was by far and away the most beautiful woman in the room, thought Jack. And she was the most beautiful pregnant woman he'd ever seen in his life.

He seemed to be enjoying this all so much that sometimes Sarah thought he'd be happy to see her remain in this state for ever. As long as they could have the baby as well, of course.

He was pleased he'd managed not to miss too much of the session.

The classroom was decorated with posters, some of them hand-drawn in felt tip by the physiotherapist. Some of them rather graphic. They fascinated Jack, and he thought he might knock up a few himself, at home.

Every window-ledge was decked with outrageously ebullient spider plants. Those plants that send out strange tendrils with miniature versions of themselves at the ends. All the spider plants here had given birth to great broods and their offspring dangled like satellites from umbilical roots.

The group was led by Ms Winthrop, a woman nearing retirement, but still of great energy, who took no nonsense whatsoever from her 'young couples'. She ruled them with an iron will and a slightly gammy leg.

They had very quickly formed themselves into a 'class'

for her. Complete with a couple who couldn't keep up with the rest, and a couple who'd become the class swots. The swots had been awarded with the prize of being able to call Ms Winthrop by her first name, Diana. It was a cause of jealousy among many of them.

Liza and Terry Parsons, the slow ones, managed a dry cleaning shop, and tended to chew gum. A habit they must have developed in the long waits between cycles, thought Jack. Liza was terribly nervous before sessions and would run through the last lesson again with Jack and Sarah by catching them in the hallway. Terry was a man who had such enormous hands that it looked as if a new baby would get lost in them. He offered Jack deals on second-hand suits that people had failed to collect. He never quite knew how to respond.

Mary and Joe had been trying for a 'miracle' for some years. Now that it had finally happened, it seemed rather a shock to them. They simply weren't prepared for the 'radical-life-adjustment' that it'd bring. They owned an organic cheese shop in Islington High Street, and quite naturally were the most mature of all the couples. They invariably smelled of cheese and were forever inviting Jack and Sarah to 'after-hours' tastings in the shop. Sarah had put paid to any further advances from them, though. Mary was thinking of going for a natural birth. She'd asked Sarah if she would stoop to accepting the drugs. Sarah replied without hesitation. 'I'm having them in the taxi.'

Jack had laughed his head off.

For Josiah and Simone, the class swots (both something in public relations), this was their second baby. So they were experts. Whenever Ms Winthrop began a new exercise they'd pipe in, 'Ah, yes, thought we'd be getting to this about now.' They'd frown and shake their heads at Liza and Terry, the slow couple. For them Jack reserved a particular dislike. Josiah brewed his own real ale, and would sit there with his hands clasped over his considerable beer gut, in imitation of his wife.

Jack looked up at Ms Winthrop, who was back in full flow.

'. . . And the contraction's gone. And sigh . . .' she said, breathily. The other couples relaxed. But not Jack and Sarah.

'You're supposed to count when I breathe in,' said Sarah under her breath to Jack. He looked into her eyes, what on earth did she mean?

'*You*'re supposed to breathe in when *I* count . . .' he said in reply.

Sarah gave out a genuine sigh.

'This is never going to work,' she said.

Ms Winthrop addressed the class calmly. 'Very good. All right, let's have another go at pushing. Remember, right down through your bottom. Men as well.'

Out of the corner of his eye Jack could see Liza and Terry as they pushed with their bottoms. Liza was really very petite and her bottom-pushing was awfully half-hearted, as if she was secretly trying to remove a peanut from her seat. Perhaps she was embarrassed. Jack felt that actual birth was going to be a terrible shock to her. He was momentarily distracted.

'Come on, Jack. Come on, there's no need to be embarrassed,' said Ms Winthrop.

Sarah smiled wryly. None of this embarrassed Jack in the least. Not only did the thought of having a baby thrill him, so did all the medical details too. The things about it that appalled her, perversely delighted him. He didn't

17

appear to have any idea that she found quite a lot of it rather undignified, but then he wasn't the one having a baby. Not that you could convince him of that.

Sometimes, when she was tired, or feeling nervous, she was convinced that he was trying to torture her with all the lurid details. Only the night before she'd caught him with her doctor's notes, which she'd hidden from him. She'd heard him muttering.

'Blood pressure's up ... urine's clear ... oedema worse ...'

She couldn't believe it and she'd rounded on him.

'You're looking at my notes!'

He'd tried bare-facedly to deny it.

'They're for my benefit, Jack, not a part-time course in obstetrics for you.'

'I'm only showing an interest,' he'd had the gall to say back.

'Bullshit. You just can't bear not being the centre of attention.'

He'd pouted and sunk into an armchair.

'I shall ignore that remark on account of your hormones.'

Then he picked up one of the pregnancy books and read out one of the chapter headings with glee.

'Dilation of the cervix!'

She took the book and hit him with it. He was torturing her with medical books.

'Good, that's it,' said Ms Winthrop, turning to Jack again. 'Think pain and then push down. Pushing the pain away. Don't forget to breathe.'

Sarah glared at him.

Jack's face took on a look of agony.

The crisp January light was gently fading in the room as Ms Winthrop paced between them, calmly counting.

Suddenly an unearthly scream shattered the air. Jack was gripping his sides in pain. He began rocking on his chair, his eyes bulging wildly. Everyone turned instantly to look at him. The class stopped dead.

'Jack, are you all right? What's wrong?' asked Ms Winthrop. Jack's screams increased as he toppled from his plastic chair into the centre of the room, where he writhed on the carpet. He was breathing in great gutfulls and gasping. Then he began to shout, 'Oh no . . . oh God . . . no . . . no . . . no! No one said it would be like this! Help me, help me. . . . !'

Liza's face was a picture. Mary was suddenly terror-struck. Josiah was catching flies.

'What's wrong with him?' Ms Winthrop asked, looking helplessly at Sarah.

'Oh God. . . !' yelled Jack. 'Give me an . . . EPIDURAL!!'

'It would appear,' said Sarah, sitting quite calmly and looking up at Ms Winthrop, 'that he's gone into labour.'

With a deft, and well-practised action, Sarah brought her foot swiftly to his balls. Jack took a sharp intake of breath and groaned in genuine pain. Sarah looked up, smiling sweetly to the dumbfounded group. The men in the room all crossed their legs.

The drive home took them past late-night shopping at Mothercare. Jack was rather pleased with himself. Mothercare late nights were currently irresistible to Jack; he regarded the baby as the most glorious shopping opportunity.

'Come on,' said Jack as he pulled up outside the store, 'we've still got loads of things to get. Essentials . . .'

'Like the rocket launcher you were looking at in Hamleys?'

'No. Don't be daft. That's for six to eights, we don't need that yet. Oh come on, let's take a spin round Mothercare.'

Sarah smiled. He was obviously building up to another outburst and she couldn't be doing with it in Mothercare.

'You go in. I'm tired and my feet are killing me. You go round, I'll wait in the car. Surprise me.'

He smiled and jumped excitedly out of the car, skipping with the other mothers into the shop. He simply couldn't understand why some of the prospective fathers in the store looked so bored, and hung back, taking idle glances at the extremely slim young assistants. Not when there was all this. Rows and rows of wonderfully clean bright objects ranged before him. Fluffy battery-operated puppies that walked towards you with big brown eyes, begged, and did a back flip. There was the most wonderful parrot too, with a mechanical beak. Whatever you said to it, it repeated.

'Pieces of eight,' said Jack.

'Pieces of eight,' repeated the toy. Jack leaned in closer. 'Piece of shit . . .' he whispered.

'Piece of shit, piece of shit, piece of shit . . .' shouted the parrot. A young woman beside him, examining one of the parrots stared at him.

'Must be made in Korea,' said Jack.

He took himself off to look at the sterilisers. Even these were interesting. The range was incredible. You could probably never have enough of such things, so he pulled out the very biggest, with the largest range of accessories and dropped it into his basket. There were bibs, and drip tray type things, all of them essential, and into his basket they went. Sanitary towels, they'd be needing them too, and musical feeding bowls.

He stood in the queue with the other mothers. He looked through his basket. There was something else, he was sure he'd missed something.

'Just a moment,' he said, laying his basket down on the cash desk.

He erupted back into the street and shouted, 'Do you need nipple pads and nipple shields or is it just the pads?'

As everyone in the street turned to look, Sarah, sitting in the car on the other side of the street, gradually descended in her seat.

'Bastard,' she muttered.

'Flesh-coloured or white?' came across the street at the top of Jack's voice.

'If your father carries on like this, we're going to be a single-parent family,' she said to her belly.

Two minutes later the rear door of the car opened and Jack piled his trophies in. People passing in the street still seemed to be watching his every move. He got into the car and sat beside her. He had a pair of plastic pants on his head.

Sarah took in a deep breath.

'I'm not embarrassed. You don't embarrass me at all any more. You can do whatever you like in Mothercare, it doesn't embarrass me any more.'

'Good,' said Jack. 'We wouldn't want you to be embarrassed.'

He turned to kiss her. Now she saw that he was wearing two plastic nipple shields on his eyes as monocles.

She held him with a steely gaze in her eyes. For a

moment, just a moment, there seemed almost to be a look of worry on his face. Almost as if he realised he'd overstepped the mark on this occasion. She enjoyed the novelty of the moment, and gently raised her hand as he flinched. Then she stroked his cheek and began to laugh. He was the most impossible boy. It could never be said, she reminded herself, that their marriage was dull. With plastic pants on his head, didn't he look handsome for her?

'You're beautiful. I love you very, very much,' he said to her softly. They slid their arms around each other and kissed.

'Come on,' said Sarah, 'we don't want to get clamped.' They laughed all the way home, doing impressions of the awful Josiah, the nervous Liza and the dreadful Joe.

'I think I certainly managed to break the ice this week, though,' said Jack.

'Mmm, and your waters . . .'

They were perfectly happy. Even though the new house was taking for ever, their lives were coming together now in a way they'd never thought possible. As they watched other people trudging through the streets, heads down, full of woe, it seemed almost unfair that they could be quite so happy. Even if, in the pre-natal class, Sarah had come very, very close to murdering him.

3

The offices of West, West & Purnell, where Jack was a partner, were just off Finsbury Circus. It was a land of brasseries and briefs, grand eighteenth-century Wren-style buildings, and modern glass and metal structures that shouted 'Corporate Image'.

The interior of WW&P was filled with swathes of expensive carpet, with the company logo woven in, and lengths of aggressive abstract art. Everywhere was polished steel and engraved glass divisions.

There were ten partners in all, all male except for Anna, the managing partner, a formidable woman of thirty-seven.

Anna was chairing the partners' meeting. She sat at the head of the long boardroom table. Her fine features, perfect make-up, and expensively groomed brunette hair were reflected in the hard polish of the mahogany. She was a very fine-looking woman and her formidable unapproachableness inspired outrageous sexual fant-asies in the older male partners, which they dared to share with each other in the gents' washroom. The older men had found it tough to accept a woman at the head of the firm and this little game perhaps alleviated the strain of it for them, schoolboyish though it was.

They'd got to the end of their meeting and Jack had raised the subject of the impending birth.

'All I'm saying,' said Anna, in the flat, authoritative tone she used for everything, 'is that if you'd like some time off around the twenty-second, a couple of days there would be good for us.'

'But Sarah's not due until the twenty-seventh, Anna,' he said, attempting to employ the same flat businesslike tone. As if this were just another case they were trying to squeeze on to a barrister's list.

'Well, that's fine,' said Anna. 'I'm just saying things will be more manageable around the twenty-second . . .' Jack's face changed.

There was a definite silence around the table as the other partners found things of interest in their Filofaxes and out of the window. There was the chance of an explosion. Anna could be the most incredibly insensitive person sometimes, and although she was certainly not 'one of the boys', at times she didn't seem to be entirely a woman either.

'Right, sure, sure,' said Jack at last. 'I'll ask Sarah to check her diary and see if she can bring the birth forward.'

'Good,' said Anna. 'That's good. Now, everyone . . .' she said, moving on to address the table, 'don't forget the partners' dinner on the third of next month. As discussed, wives are not invited.' The men nodded. Jack was still shaking his head in disbelief.

Later that afternoon Jack put his head around her office door.

'Jack!' she said brightly.

'I've just seen the memo you sent me.'

'Memo?'

'Yes, um, how did you head it, ah, yes "– Clarification of Contract".'

24

'Ah, you got it, good.'

Not that your memo doesn't fully clarify the situation, Anna, but two days? Two days paternity leave?'

'Yes, is there a problem?'

'Not at all, I just want to get it perfectly clear in my mind why it's two whole days. Presumably one for the actual birth, and the other for, for what, buying the nappies, I suppose.'

'Well, obviously Jack you're free to use them however you feel.'

'Amazing. You know, every time I have doubts about the generosity of this firm something like this comes along and just bowls me over. It happens so often it makes me dizzy.'

'Good, I'm glad you can see it from our side.'

'Naturally.' Jack spun on his heels. Then he stopped himself and laid his hand on her office door. 'Tell me,' he said. 'If I have twins, do I get four days?'

Anna held him with her eyes for a moment and sighed.

'Jack, you know as well as I, that as partnerships go, we really are most flexible. Most flexible . . .'

'Just the word I'd have chosen,' said Jack.

Nathaniel was having a little difficulty with choosing the right words this afternoon as well. He was sure nine across was correct but he was buggered if he could get thirteen down. It was no use asking his men either, they were good men but the written side of life was not their forte. He gave up on the crossword and turned back to the news pages. He never failed to be astonished by the things he read, the life that spread before him, in the pages of the London *Evening Standard*. Cripplingly sad stories of personal loss, infuriating accounts of corruption at the very highest level. Building projects constantly held up by government incompetence and filibustering. The widespread corruption in this city appalled him. No wonder nothing ever seemed to be achieved by this most ineffectual of administrations. He shook his head and reached for another stiffening gulp of tea.

He looked around the room for a moment. When the dado rails were reinstalled, and the doors rehung, and that bloody great hole filled in, this really would be a very fine room. It would be a credit to their painstaking craftsmanship. Nathaniel was just about to lay down his mug and bring his men in to make that final assault on the dining-room, when a most astonishing story caught his eye. There had been an episode, this morning, on the eight-twenty into Waterloo. A British Rail guard had suddenly gone berserk and had begun wandering the carriages switching all the lights on and off. Then he had begun throwing commuters' briefcases out of the windows on to the trackside. A union spokesman, quoted in full by the paper, had said that, considering the stress railway workers now laboured under, 'scenes like this on commuter trains would become a commonplace occurrence'. Nathaniel shook his head again. How could these people live like this? How could they shuttle into the big city, day in and day out, canned up like sardines, and sit at their nine-to-five jobs? Nathaniel's profession had made him something of a philosopher. When it came down to it, what was life really for? he asked himself. How could people bare to go on in this mundane way, tied, like himself, to the constant drudgery of work, work, work. Never a moment's genuine peace and relaxation.

Suddenly the air was broken with the watchman's whistle from the roof. Bugger! He threw the paper down and picked up the architects' drawings. Jack was pulling up outside with his young and very pregnant wife.

'OK, lads,' he said, 'let's get that bloody old bath up the stairs. Look like we're doing something.'

Most of the scaffolding had now come down and the orange tarpaulin had been lifted from the roof. Rather than being a sign of progress it served only to illustrate, to the rest of the square, how far Nathaniel and his men had gone to destroy this fine house.

He barked some orders at his men. 'Your end up a bit, watch it, watch it, electrics at three o'clock.' And the men were responding with suitable grunts and moans. Jack spotted the early edition of the *Evening Standard* lying open on the floor. He wasn't impressed.

Sarah stood behind him. She hadn't visited the house for a week, and was visibly shocked to see that it was nowhere near habitable. They were due to be moving into the house in three days and had brought with them some of the breakables that they didn't trust to the removal men. Jack laid down a box of antique crystal glasses, and looked forlornly around him.

He tried to give Sarah a look of reassurance, but it wasn't an easy one to pull off. He dashed up the stairs after Nathaniel.

Jack braced himself. This time there'd be no debate about it, no excuses about the structural instabilities caused by the blitz . . . no more blaming the Romans for siting London on a bed of clay, or cowboy Edwardians, or Hitler. This time Nathaniel himself was to take the blame.

'Nathaniel, this is our third attempt to move into this house and this time, this time, you aren't going to stop us . . .' Nathaniel stared at him, expressionless. '. . . We are moving here in three days' time whether you want us to or not.'

Nathaniel's face remained impassive as Jack and he, and three of his men, hovered on the stairway, with the bath between them.

Nathaniel began to nod slowly, in the conciliatory way of a cornered man.

'Could work the weekend . . .' he said. 'Mean extra men of course . . .'

'Right, good,' said Jack, and turned on the stairs before that little nervous twitch returned. 'And don't expect me to pay for them!' Jack marched boldly back down the stairs.

Behind him, out of earshot, Nathaniel was muttering under his breath: 'You already have, mate, several times over . . .'

Jack was hyperventilating ever so slightly when they got out into the square. They stood with the skip behind them, surveying the wreckage of the house.

'That told 'em,' said Jack.

'Certainly did, darling.'

'It's just a question of being firm, gaining their respect'. He felt the warmth of her hand on his shoulder. 'Mind you, having said that, I sometimes think it would be easier for them if we didn't move in at all.'

'Come on, let's get going,' said Sarah, her voice coming from further down the street, where she stood by the car. The reassuring hand was still lying heavy on his shoulder. When Jack turned his head to look he saw that it was also rather hairy, and wearing black woollen gloves with the fingers cut off. Out of the skip a head emerged. Wearing a sort of black plastic hat, with fur-lined ear flaps that gave the rugged and dishevelled face the look of an old

28

Labrador. He used Jack's shoulder to pull himself up out of the debris.

'Could you possibly spare the price of a warming cup of tea?' he asked politely. Jack looked towards Sarah for a moment, almost as if this were her fault, and turned sharply back to the tramp.

'Get out of my skip!'

The tramp looked rather shocked and stood up to his full height among the planks and plasterboard.

'I was here first!' he said.

'It's my skip!' growled Jack.

The tramp removed his hand from Jack's shoulder. 'Possession,' he declared, 'is nine-tenths of the law.'

Jack pulled away. Not only didn't he seem to be master of his own house anymore, he wasn't even master of the skip outside. He marched himself silently to the car and got in with Sarah. Things were not going at all well with the new house.

Three days later, Jack watched the removal van with all their worldly goods in it pull away from their old house in Hammersmith. They were following on in the car after the men had had a chance to get started, and after they'd had time to say something of a farewell to the old place alone. Anna, the senior partner, had recommended 'her' removal company, and like her, they'd been rather swift and silent.

Well, thought Jack to himself, I've stuck to my guns. It had been three days since his ultimatum to Nathaniel, and here they were, moving at last.

He looked up at the small terraced house in Hammersmith that had been their home since before they'd married. He smiled at it. It'd been a happy 'first house'. It

29

seemed awfully small now to have been the stage on which all the dramas of their first years together had been set. When they'd first moved in, their friends had dubbed it 'The Orphanage', because it was a perpetual open house to everyone, old school friends, university chums, neighbours, anyone at a loss for Sunday lunch. It was during one of Sarah's vast Sunday lunches, generally served from tureens laid on the living-room floor, with their friends sitting on cushions, that he had proposed to her.

He'd gone down on one knee while she made a pint of gravy in the kitchen. He remembered how she'd held on to his shoulders and laughed, while a tear ran down her cheek and she'd simply replied, 'You're pissed.'

Jack walked back into the empty house. There were pale squares on the hallway walls where pictures of his college eights had been, and a long narrow strip where his school photograph had hung. It was rather sad. There were the marks on the bare boards of the stairs from when he'd gone to the off-licence and left the bath running; and there was the dent in the banister from the brass ashtray that Sarah had thrown at him. It was kind of sad that they'd never see these small things again to remind them of the early incidents of their lives. He was already forming a dislike for the pleasant young couple who had bought the place from them. It would never be their house really, not in the way that it had been his and Sarah's.

Jack laughed and snapped himself out of it. Of course it wasn't sad at all. They'd had great times, and now they had a great new house with a nursery to decorate. It was an exciting day. He spun into the bare-boarded living-room. Only a small portable stereo remained in the room.

Jack bent over to pull the plug from the wall. Sarah was sitting on the floor, leaning against the wall. He turned to look at her.

She was sobbing. She looked up, and around the room. Her shoulders were gently rising and falling. This house had meant so much to her, it almost seemed to embody the nature of their lives together, or at least, the nature of that life up until now. There was an uncomplicated feel to it, a spontaneity. Like their dreadful attempts at rag-rolling in the bathroom, and the missing louvres from the wardrobe that had never been replaced. First-house simplicity that could never be tasted again.

Jack switched the tape player on. The cassette played one of those songs that had been a backdrop to so much that this house had been and Mick Hucknell's voice filled the room with 'Stars'.

She looked up at Jack, smiling while her tears increased. They slowly rose in each other's arms and began to shuffle around, dancing across the creaking boards, through the shafts of January sun. The tinny sound of the cassette echoed throughout the house.

'This is where it all starts, darling . . . this is where it all starts,' he said softly.

4

'I thought you said Monday week,' said Nathaniel.

'You know what I said, and here we are. We're moving in and you're moving out.'

It was chaos in the Islington house. Sarah left Jack to his 'debate' with Nathaniel and lay on her back with her legs up against the wall to relieve the ache in her swollen feet. The dancing hadn't helped.

Nathaniel seemed absolutely astonished that they intended moving in. He'd laughed when he saw the removal van arrive earlier and had insisted that they must have got the wrong house. For some time they were all too ready to believe him.

Nathaniel was practically treating them as intruders in their own house. But Jack had quite got into his stride now when it came to Nathaniel.

Sarah sighed and tried to smile. The room was a complete mess, what the hell had the builders been doing? She tried to cheer up by reminding herself of her mother's favourite advice about decorating. It was always best to live in a place first, before doing it up. But, then, her mother's house never had been done up, it was just as it was when she'd moved in in 1968.

Sarah could hear Nathaniel following hard behind Jack as he paced about the house directing the removal men with their boxes.

All the boxes had been rather optimistically marked with labels like 'Dining-room', 'Master Bedroom', 'Nursery'. Which in this kind of dereliction was no help to them whatsoever.

Nathaniel, paradoxically, was protesting that the house wasn't quite yet up to his own high standards.

'Then you'll just have to come back, won't you?' snapped Jack.

'But it'll only take a couple more days,' said Nathaniel, sounding as if Jack was being outrageously unreasonable about it all.

Jack looked at him hard. How could he possibly estimate the work at just a couple more days? They'd already had those days and it was just as it was before. 'Tough,' said Jack.

The telephone, on the floor beside Sarah, rang. She reached out and picked up the receiver. It was Rob, one of their oldest friends, and a colleague of Jack's at West, West & Purnell.

At the end of the call Sarah slapped the floor in annoyance. Jack walked back in, Nathaniel still at his heels with a look of offended annoyance on his face, flapping about with his plans. How dare these young people just tip up like this and take over his domain, messing it all up with tea chests and furniture. And talk of changing the colour of the walls.

'Tell me it isn't true,' she said. 'Jack, tell me you haven't invited Rob and Lizzie over for dinner tonight.'

He swung round. What was she talking about?

'No, of course I haven't, not tonight,' he said with absolute certainty and distracted by Nathaniel following him about like a yapping, disgruntled dog.

'So why do they think they're coming for dinner with Nick and Diane and Pamela?'

'Gosh, all our friends?'

Sarah narrowed her eyes and slowly slid her legs down from the wall. 'Jack!'

'Well I don't know. You know what Rob's like . . .' Then his face began to change from the expression of controlled assertiveness he'd been using with Nathaniel to one of relieved amusement at Rob's mistake. 'Oh, yes, yes I do. Rob's got it wrong. It's next week. I did invite them, yes, but they're coming a week after we move in. Not today, a week after.'

Suddenly Nathaniel began a slow, guilty move away from him and Jack's face took on a nasty blackness. He turned to Nathaniel.

'We should have moved in last week, shouldn't we?' he said, looking like he could easily take a swing at him.

Nathaniel's hands flapped about again with the architects' blueprints and he suddenly seemed to need to attend to something in the hallway. Then, quietly, he let himself out and escaped into the square.

They had to face the fact that their friends were coming over for dinner that evening. He could see she was really very distraught about the prospect.

'Look, I'll cook,' said Jack. 'It'll be fine, I'll cook.'

Sarah propped her head against the wall and let out a groan of pain. 'It's not fair. Look at me, I'm just one big swelling, I look disgusting . . .'

'Sarah . . .' he said, trying to be supportive. But God, he suddenly wished for their old, small, house in Hammersmith, and those last moments there where they'd shuffled across the floor to a tape cassette. Sarah turned from the wall.

'And you know damn well I'll end up doing it all and you'll end up getting pissed and boring everyone stupid so we won't see them all again for six months.'

'Sweetheart, I'll cook. I promise I'll cook.'

The new house was silent around them now. Nathaniel had disappeared, the removal men had gone. They were alone in what felt an overlarge, unwelcoming house, having their first row. It had taken them, what? Fifteen minutes, half an hour maybe at best, and now they stood, opposed in the wreckage of their dreamhouse.

That evening they improvised a dining table for their friends from a line of upturned tea chests. For a dinner service they had an array of aluminium trays with cardboard lids. Jack's promise to cook, of course, had consisted of sending a taxi to the local Chinese take-away.

On arrival their friends had been visibly shocked. They tried their best, but couldn't help but be only marginally encouraging with comments like, 'It's certainly got character', and worse, 'It has potential'. They all seemed to be missing the old dinner parties they had enjoyed in Hammersmith already.

Conversation naturally turned to the baby.

'Of course, you know what it'll be from now on,' said Rob, Jack's best friend at WW&P. 'You can forget any plans to go to the rugby with me once you've got kids, Jack.' Then he turned to Sarah. 'And it'll be mums' coffee mornings for you in a couple of weeks. And you'll be chewing rusks for lunch.'

'I'd rather die,' said Sarah.

Sarah's younger sister, Pamela, leaned her head on her hand and stared doe-eyed at Jack, her wonderful brother-in-law. 'I think Jack'll make a fabulous father,' she said slowly.

Sarah laughed out loud. 'He won't, he'll be dreadful. He's too selfish.'

Jack suddenly looked like a nine-year-old again, accused of cheating at Monopoly.

'Oh, don't look so hurt,' said Sarah. 'It was a joke. But you are, you know.'

'I'll tell you what he's going to be,' said Rob, laying down his glass of Chianti among the aluminium trays and stray straw mushrooms. 'He's going to be another baby bore.'

Jack steadied himself. He'd been attacked. Sarah moved the large tray of noodles away from him in case he dumped it on Rob's head.

'I resent that,' said Jack.

'Well it's true.'

'I am not going to be another baby bore. I am going to be the biggest baby bore there's ever been!'

They laughed. Sarah stroked his hair.

'You already are, darling, you already are,' she said.

After several more bottles of red wine, and quite a lot of Tiger beer, everyone was truly beginning to relax. For the first time Sarah, who wasn't drinking, began to imagine that perhaps things weren't so different after all. Jack was talking animatedly and jumping around the room, recreating for everyone his going-into-labour incident at the pre-natal class. Then he went to find the plastic pants and the nipple shields and did the Mothercare episode for them.

Tears of laughter were streaming down their faces as he burst back into the room after rummaging for a few moments upstairs. He was wearing Sarah's lipstick, one of her biggest polka dot dresses, and with a pillow stuffed up his front.

Then he lay on the floor, howled and gave birth to the parrot that shrieked 'piece of shit, piece of shit, piece of shit'.

He flopped down beside Sarah with a gleeful look on his wicked face.

Sarah put her arm around him. Maybe this house, and this new life wasn't so frightening after all. How could a change of address ever change them? They would always be the same. Unstoppable.

It had been an exhausting day for both of them, and very long. In the last hour, as well, Jack had polished off a whole bottle of Chianti to himself. The mix of this and the Tiger beer was beginning to have a pretty lethal effect on him. He was actually speaking Italian Chinese.

'I think this is one boy who needs his sleep,' said Sarah. He laid his head on her bosom, nuzzling her contentedly and trying to contain his hiccups. As he reached out, blindly, for the litre bottle of wine she pulled his hand back.

'You really will be the most awful father,' she whispered into his ear and kissed him.

Their friends went home after Rob and Pamela had helped get Jack up the stairs.

Sarah came out of the bathroom. Her husband was sprawled on the bed, trousers half on, half off, like someone who'd fallen headlong in mud. Her polka dot dress was still on the landing. The evening had been exhausting for her and she levered up her side of the duvet and slid herself in on her back. Jack picked up his head momentarily.

'Baby's got hiccups,' she said.

Jack's voice sunk deep into the duck down of the duvet. 'Oh God. It's going to be a drunk just like its father,' he said. Sarah smiled. Jack was such a drama queen. He loved to picture himself as an awful drunk but it was all just an excuse to behave badly and claim that he'd forgotten the awful things he'd got up to. She thought of her younger sister's comment that he'd make a wonderful father. He would. She smiled as she remembered that doe-eyed look in Pamela's eyes.

'Pamela's got a crush on you, you know,' she said.

'Of course she has,' he said. 'She's your sister. It runs in the family.' His arm seemed to be involuntarily flapping about for the Chianti bottle again. She kissed his head just above his ear.

'Switch out the light,' she said.

Jack reached out. He loved her. He'd do anything for her. He thrust out his arm. And fell off the bed.

He was too tired, and too pissed to bother right now with hauling himself back up on to the bed. From his uneasy place on the floor his right arm flapped in the air until he found the light. Click. Sarah lay back and closed her eyes, certain that her husband was quite comfortable where he was, nose on carpet. She was in no condition to heave him up.

She lay for a while. The square was perfectly quiet, not like Hammersmith where she could hear the sound of the underground and the traffic on the Broadway, people singing in the streets as they piled out of the Palais. But here it was peaceful, the square like a little haven in the middle of London. Perhaps only the sound of that rather dignified old tramp, walking the street outside and muttering, no, perhaps not muttering, more like recitation. Poetry perhaps. She didn't know. Tonight she was restless, twinges within her body disturbed her, but her body had felt so universally odd over the last nine months that nothing was physically new anymore at all. She felt so physically unreal most of the time nothing surprised her any longer.

Though the heating wasn't properly programmed there was sweat on her brow. She concentrated on Jack's snoring from the floor, it was something to fix upon. There were no curtains at the window and the moon seemed to be racing through the sky as the clouds skidded across it. It looked impatient for the next day, to have done and be gone. She was impatient for the next day too. Another day, another ante-natal class, another day of swollen feet.

She looked up at the alien room. How many years would they spend together here? How many other children would be conceived?

It was no use, all this thinking. She was exhausted after the events of the day, it was just her brain down-loading. Her eyelids began to flap and she fell, very suddenly, into a deep, deep sleep.

She slept peacefully for a couple of hours but then woke with a start again. She had the most terrible indigestion. She reached for the lightswitch and looked at her watch. This indigestion was swiftly getting worse. This was certainly more than a twinge, but, oh, no, it couldn't be. Not now, surely? She wasn't ready, but oh, my God, oh Jack, oh shit, this was what all the practice was about. She held her watch under the bedside lamp and stared at the second hand. Time went for ever round until six minutes, every six minutes. It couldn't be. She was excited, frightened. She reached her arm out for Jack.

Of course, he was asleep on the floor, she remembered. She quickly became very lucid indeed, as if it was some sort of natural survival mechanism. A survival mode, the key to which was 'don't panic Jack . . . speak to him calmly, wake him gently, get him to drive the car, call a taxi, do whatever. Try to slow down my breathing. Don't panic Jack, don't panic Jack . . .'

'Jack . . . Jack . . .' called Sarah gently. 'Jack?'

There was a rustle from the floor.

'Yep?'

'Jack, I want you to stay calm . . . but could you take me to the hospital please?'

There was a silence that lasted for ever. Jack could feel the carpet tickling his nose and wondered why it presumed to do so. Half-awake, he began to speak.

'Hospital . . . yep . . . OK . . .'

He was being calm, she thought, this is good, we're half-way there. Then he seemed to go back to sleep.

Suddenly he shot up from the floor, one arm in his shirt, one arm out. His trousers still around his ankles.

'Hospital!!'

'Jack, stay calm . . .'

'What's wrong, are you ill?'

'The baby's coming,' said Sarah.

'The baby's coming. What, now? The baby's coming now? Are you contracting? You're having contractions?'

Something from the lessons had sunk in, but there was already an air of panic to his voice.

'Every six minutes.'

'Shit, shit!' screamed Jack.

'Just calm down. Did you pack the bag?'

'No.'

'Jack . . .'

40

'I'll do it now. It was packed, then it got unpacked. During the packing . . .'

Jack reached for a large book, the pregnancy book, that was lying by the bedside. He'd insisted that the removal men bring it to this room. He began flicking frantically through the pages, like a child who'd scribbled stickmen in the corner of each page.

'What are you doing?'

Jack stopped dead, and the book froze.

'I don't know,' he said. 'I don't know.' The air of panic was increasing.

Sarah breathed in, held her stomach, and turned to him with what she hoped was a simple, everyday expression on her face.

'Jack, stop panicking,' she said firmly.

'I'm not panicking. I've rehearsed this for months. I'm in complete control.'

'Jack, pack the bag and call a taxi.'

Jack was dithering, and spinning around on the spot.

'Right . . . yep . . .' he said, rerunning her instructions in his head. He began battling with the errant trouser leg and the other arm of his shirt, trying to dress.

'One, two, three, . . . one, two, three . . .' He was muttering.

Bag. Taxi. He reminded himself, he got to the head of the stairs. Where in Hammersmith the landing would have veered left, before its narrow fearsome descent, so here it turned right, and, woken in the night, and in panic, Jack's legs thought he was still in the old house. Headlong he went, with a resounding crash, still with his trousers undone, down the flight of stairs. His body turned him at the first level. He cracked his head against the bottom banister and knocked himself soundly out.

There was just a whimper from him before he lost consciousness.

'Jack! Jack. . . !' called Sarah.

It was an interminable wait but when the paramedics did arrive they were most understanding, although a little unsure at first as to which of them was the most immediate emergency.

The paramedic held the gas to Sarah's mouth.

'Are you all right?' he asked, in that immediately friendly tone that all medical people have in emergencies.

'Yes . . .'

'Having another one?'

'Just going,' said Sarah, bravely, not wanting to be any more trouble tonight than these things surely are.

'Good . . .' He patted her hand.

'I just hope he doesn't miss it. He'll never forgive himself . . .'

Sarah, from her position, sitting at the back of the ambulance, clutching the face mask, looked at Jack, lying unconscious on the stretcher, his face white and cold. Out like a light.

5

Margaret and Michael sat beside Jack's bed in the hospital. He lay there motionless, his face was drained of blood and his arms were rigid by his sides.

It was the middle of the night. A handkerchief was damp in Margaret's hands, and her mascara streaked down her face as she stared down at her stricken son. Michael, Jack's father, sat on the other side of the bed, as silent as ever. His head was bent over a polystyrene cup which he picked slowly to pieces, dropping centimetre-sized squares of it on to the green lino.

A nurse appeared with the offer of more tea from a machine. Margaret glanced toward the mess her husband had made of his last cup.

'No, no thank you,' she said. 'No more tea.'

The nurse left them alone again. This part of the hospital was quiet. Casualty had been a nightmare, people yelling with minor cuts and bruises, yobs complaining with dislocated shoulders from street brawls. She had despised them, and their petty, un-necessary miseries. Real drama, real tragedy, took place in a quiet stillness, like this. Plain green curtains had been pulled around them as they sat through the night. They were the slowest hours.

Margaret wouldn't have wanted anyone to have seen her this way. Ordinarily she would have fussed in her dressing-room for hours. Experimenting with combinations of beige twin sets and strings of pearls. She still had the sort of manners, and the approach to life, that would have blended easily at a dinner-dance in the 1950s. Her greatest, and almost all-consuming, passion for the last fifteen years had been bridge, which she played with adept viciousness every Thursday evening without fail.

Drama like this didn't enter her world. But tonight she ached for her son, she wanted to pull him into her arms, and kiss away the pain as she'd done after a scraped knee when he was her little boy.

At five in the morning, when the rattling sound of the morning tea trolleys began in the long corridors, Jack began to stir. Margaret held his hand. He groaned as she touched him. Then he opened his eyes. He saw his father, his great white, silent, head leaning towards him. He saw his mother. He didn't understand. Why were they here beside him, looking so drained?

'What is it. . . ? what's wrong . . .? Mum?'

Margaret began to cry. His hand shook as she gripped it harder and harder and tears ran down her powdered cheeks.

'Oh Jack . . .' she said. Her voice was cracked and breathless, and filled with desperation. His father laid his hand on the pillow beside his head.

'It's Sarah, Jack . . .' said his father.

'What? Sarah, it's what?'

Jack leapt up from the bed and tore at the curtains. He began to run through the ward, leaving his parents and their awful news behind him. His thoughts were in absolute confusion, and he ran like someone fleeing a fire. His face was panic-stricken, his eyes staring straight ahead of him.

The hospital was vast with endless corridors, and everywhere it was smooth and clean and ramped. There were harsh overhead lights that picked out every speck of dust or pain. He followed the arrows and the signs to the maternity department and came to a halt in a starkly bare waiting area.

There, hunched in a corner, were people he knew. Sarah's mother, Phil. Sarah's young sister, Pamela. Where was Sarah?

Pamela looked up, her eyes red and streaming, her hair a mess. She looked entirely lost. Phil pulled herself up from her chair and staggered towards him. She looked all cried out, but on seeing Jack her whole body began to shake again. He held on to her.

'Oh Jack,' she said. 'My girl . . . my little girl . . .'

Jack was shown into a small room. Sarah lay on a bed, no pillow under her head, her hands folded across her chest. Her eyes were closed, she looked asleep except for the fact that no-one could sleep this soundly. It couldn't be so. Jack looked around the room frantically, surely there was another Sarah somewhere, smiling and laughing, fussing about with something. There was nothing in the room at all, no equipment, no pictures, nothing but Sarah, lying in a bed too perfectly made. Surely someone would come in and say there'd been a dreadful mistake, that none of this was true. They had to, it was impossible. Sarah was so alive, so trusting, so resilient to everything. It was impossible that she was dead.

He collapsed beside her, lying his head next to hers. A small trickle of water ran slowly from one of her eyes. A tear. She was crying, thought Jack. She must be alive if she was crying. Then Jack realised that the tear wasn't hers at all, it was his.

He laid his hand on her face but there was no response to his touch. He weaved his fingers through her perfectly combed hair. She looked so perfect it was all so unbelievable.

He lay his head on the bed beside her, his tears, warm tears splashing against her white resilient skin.

He walked back to the waiting area, his feet moving involuntarily, his limbs numb. Phil and Pamela looked up at him with their reddened eyes. No one spoke.

'I have to go,' said Jack, blankly, his eyes staring as if he couldn't see them at all.

'Yes, of course,' said Phil, quietly.

'We're having a dishwasher delivered . . .' he said.

They stood silently for a moment. Jack could barely think at all. All his mind could fix on was the banality of the delivery of their dishwasher this morning.

'Jack . . . Jack . . .' It was his mother's voice. He turned to see her. She was holding a baby. He glanced at it for moment, he took in the blanket she held the tiny thing wrapped in, he took in the green aertex hospital smock, he couldn't focus on the creature's eyes.

'It's a girl, Jack . . . a little girl,' said his mother. She smiled with tears still running, slowly now, down her mascara-scarred cheeks. Jack looked away from the baby. He didn't want to see it.

'I'm late,' said Jack, and he began to walk away from them, staring ahead. Margaret looked helplessly at Phil. Michael seemed fixed to the spot, flapping one hand ineffectually, not knowing what to do.

Jack was going. Pamela ran after him.

She led him to her car, he was like someone walking in a dream.

They began the drive to Islington. He was unable to look at Pamela and leaned his head against the cold glass of the window.

The office workers were clattering along the pavements. People were playing pop music on their car stereos, and when they stopped at traffic lights, men were laughing and rolling kegs of beer down into the cellar of a bar. How dared they? It was as if they had no knowledge that things like this could happen. Everything was the same this morning as it had been yesterday morning. Except for him.

Jack stood in the kitchen. Pamela had managed to make some coffee but they both just stood there, leaning against the worktops, nursing the mugs.

Pamela let the delivery men in. Jack watched them, as if from a great distance, from across the street, or from an observation platform, as they huffed and puffed in front of him with the dishwasher. There were two of them.

'Where would you like it?' asked one. Jack looked slowly up at him.

'Where would you like it, mate?' he said again, insistently.

'Anywhere,' said Jack. The delivery man shook his head. The kitchen was obviously integral. It could only be installed on the wet side, but since they hadn't offered him a cup of coffee he wasn't going to bother installing it anyway.

'Fair enough,' he said, and directed his mate to plonk it right in the middle of the room. They'd have a laugh about it in the van later. He reached into his back pocket and pulled out the delivery note. He waved it under Jack's nose.

'Put your moniker on this then, guv,' he said.

Jack took the paper and scrawled his name across it. Simply writing the word 'Jack'.

'Cheer up, mate, it may never happen,' said the delivery man.

Jack was too exhausted to respond. The men went.

They stayed in the kitchen for some time.

'I know there's nothing I can really do,' said Pamela, 'but if there's anything . . .'

'Why don't you call me later? You should go and look after your mother.'

'Yes, yes, I should,' said Pamela. She slowly laid her coffee cup down and looked at Jack again. He was staring at a pile of shopping leaning against the French windows. The word 'Mothercare' stung him, printed on the side of the plastic bags. There were the plastic pants, the nipple shields, the parrot that Jack had taught to swear.

'There's a load of stuff in the corner there,' he said. 'Could you take it?'

'Won't you need it . . . ?' she said. But Jack's eyes were empty and grey. He said nothing but simply turned his head away from the things, wanting nothing to do with them.

'Yes, yes of course I will,' said Pamela and she picked up the bags. She hovered for a moment, unsure whether to kiss him or not. He was staring ahead into empty space.

Pamela let herself out.

Jack turned to look out of the French windows into the garden. A layer of frost lay over the broken bags of cement, a few weedy plants struggled from the flagstones.

It was a desolate sight. He turned back into the house and began slowly wandering about it. He walked into the dining-room. The tea chests were there, the Chinese food solidifying in the aluminium trays. Cigarette stubs in ashtrays, and the smell of their friends' smoke from last night still hung in the air. It was as if their voices and their laughter were still here, echoing in the empty house. It looked like so many mornings after one of their haphazard dinner parties. The wine glasses were still in the places where they had been laid down. He flopped down beside the debris and reached out his hand.

There was Sarah's glass in front of him. He stroked the stem with his finger, and then gently folded his hand around it. He lifted it up towards his mouth.

There on the rim of the glass was a perfect imprint of Sarah's lipstick. His eyes became fixed on the impression of her lips.

As he stared at it the telephone rang. The ringing was distant as if from another room, another place. He stared at the glass. He let it ring, and then there was the faraway sound of the answer-phone clicking on. Then a voice cut through the distance like a knife, saying, 'Hello, this is Sarah. I'm afraid neither Jack or I can answer the phone right now, but please leave a message and we'll call you back as soon as possible . . .' Suddenly the numbness in his body departed and he felt intense, and physical, pain.

'. . . Hi!' said another voice, bright and outrageously filled with life. 'It's just Rob to say thanks for last night, and Jack, don't forget to let us know as soon as anything happens. Love to you both . . .' Jack's face creased with pain. He pulled himself up and shuffled over to the answering machine as it was rewinding. He hit the button, and sank down beside it as he played the recording of Sarah's message over and over again.

Jack stood up and began to stagger helplessly around the room. He grabbed hold of one of the packing-cases and threw it into a mirror that rested against the wall. He picked up the box of crystal glasses they had brought with them yesterday and he hurled them at the window, smashing the panes. He destroyed the stereo, he smashed vases on the mantelpiece, then he spilled into the living-room, trashing everything in his way. There was such an inexpressible fury in his heart. It was as if he blamed the house. He grabbed the cushions from the sofa and tried to pull them apart, until, exhausted, he collapsed, gripping them to his chest, and sobbed. Life was over.

6

Phil visited the churchyard alone. It had been two weeks since Sarah had been buried and the flowers were now brown and frost-bitten.

She had brought a small trowel with her to tidy up the grave. It was just a mound of earth, no headstone yet, just a bare, bleak heap of dying flowers.

It was a slightly dilapitated churchyard on the Brompton Road. Chelsea Football Club were playing at home today and the sound of roars and cheers filled the empty graveyard. It seemed the most awful affront, a headlong clash between the quick and the dead.

'Blue is the colour!' The voices swelled. 'Football is the game. We're all together, and winning is our aim . . .'

Phil wept.

There, next to Sarah's, was another grave, with a solid headstone and long-established moss and chrysanthemums. It was the grave of Phil's husband, Sarah's father. Phil wiped the tears from her eyes. She would have given anything to have taken up this place herself before her daughter.

It had been a large, but bleak funeral. They had all spent much of the service looking away from the priest to the church door, hoping to see Jack. But Jack didn't come. He had disappeared from the face of the earth.

Margaret was beside herself with worry about him.

Nathaniel his builder hadn't seen him since the day before Sarah's death. Pamela had been around to the house almost every day, but all she could see through the windows was debris, and the remains of the meal they had been eating on that night. The police didn't seem to want to know about it. He hadn't shown up at work.

Margaret and Michael were looking after the baby girl. In some ways, thought Phil, Margaret seemed to come into her own in a crisis. It was so bitterly unfair, all this life-having-to-go-on Britishness. Really she'd like to just throw herself headlong into the mud of her daughter's grave, but instead she'd come with a little trowel.

The home team scored.

'Blue is the colour! Football is the game. We're all together . . .'

She cleared away the last of the dead flowers. Under a pile of rotten lilies her hand hit something cold and hard. It was a whisky bottle. She shuddered, but as she set off for the bin with it, she noticed a red rose wilting inside it.

She had the sudden sense that there was someone else in the deserted churchyard and looked about her, searching through the monuments and yew trees with her eyes. She thought of Jack. There was no one there, just the bitter wind, and the rise and fall of football songs.

7

Jack had been in the square.

After trashing the house he had never wanted to see it again but now he stood blankly in the cold of the street and then headed across the road into the park.

He began to walk along its gravel paths, making aimless circuits again and again, oblivious to everything, only vaguely aware of the other people in the park. There was a pair of nannies taking their charges for a mid-morning walk, pushing them in buggies with their wheels rattling on the frost-crisp gravel. Two boys were kicking at a half-deflated football that thudded with the dull sound of rubber and air. Overhead, an executive passed in a helicopter. Jack stared up into the sky. Everything seemed distant and disconnected. He felt sick and confused. His head was thumping but the concussion he'd suffered, as well as shock, numbed his senses.

He collapsed, exhausted, behind the small gardener's hut, which was tucked under cover of a group of plane trees and hydrangeas at the centre of the square.

He didn't wake until the chill of evening roused him. Slumped against the hut beside him was another man.

'Ah, a good evening to you,' he said as Jack opened his eyes and slowly turned to focus on him. 'You appear to have stumbled across my little spot,' he said, smiling.

Jack vaguely recognised the man. He recalled

something about a man with gloves without fingers, and a fur-lined hat. But for the moment he couldn't place him and so he just stared into his face. The tramp had a gentle expression, and there was obvious concern in his eyes. He held out a bottle of whisky to Jack. The young man wasn't dressed for the street. He wore just jeans and a shirt. The shirt had blood on the collar. He'd freeze in this weather without whisky inside him.

'Care for a tot?'

Jack reached for the bottle, automatically. His hand was shaking. He took a long hard swig of the whisky. He could feel just a dull burning sensation as he poured it down his throat. As he passed the bottle back the tramp held out his hand.

'The name's William,' he said, 'and you are?'

Jack tried hard to concentrate his mind. 'Jack . . .' he mumbled.

'Delighted to make your acquaintance,' said William. His voice was refined and educated and was entirely at odds with the way he looked.

He found Jack a blanket which he had stashed behind the gardener's grass-cuttings bin. Though this young man had very little to say for himself, it was a pleasant change, William felt, to have some civil company. Teenage hooligans had come to infest the square in the early evenings lately. They drank cider on the swings in the little playground, and kicked the heads off the first of the crocuses. Then he'd hear their hoarse breaking voices heading towards him, intent on hunting him out and being vile. Shouting insults, prodding him awake, and, worst of all, pouring away his whisky. William could not abide such ill discipline.

Jack and William drank the bottle together. Then after a couple of hours Jack passed out again.

In the morning he woke to find a Scottie dog in a little tartan coat, sniffing at his face. He swiped out at it, and it dashed away, startled, back to the sound of its lead chain rattling by its master's side. Jack staggered to his feet, trying to remember where he was. He pushed his way through the undergrowth. He stood for a moment, looking beyond the oval of the park, to where the people of the other world, the suddenly unreal one, were slamming their front doors, de-icing their windscreens, and setting off to the office.

Through the branches of the hydrangea, Jack stared at them, at their suits and briefcases. They were creatures from across a divide. How absolutely pointless their morning panic seemed to him. If they felt just a small part of what he did now they would simply not bother at all. They'd leave their children, in their absurd school uniforms, where they stood. They'd forget about their smart cars and wander, like him, in despair. He turned away from them and fixed his eyes, as if mesmerised, on the branches of a tree. The branches were pinky white with the first buds of blossom just beginning to break through. It was as if the twig ends had split in the night to reveal that there was nothing inside. No sap, no life, just a blank empty whiteness at the heart of the tree.

William's hand fell on his shoulder.

'A very good morning, Jack. Slept well, I trust?' he said.

Jack turned slowly to look at him and grunted. Every bone in his body ached, his eyes were sore, and he was shaking with cold and exhaustion. William, on the other hand, looked quite bright and cheery, as if he'd spent the night on a feather bed.

'Admiring our ornamental cherry?' said William, indicating the tree. Jack looked back at it blankly.

'The Japanese confetti tree,' continued William. 'I can't say I've ever really cared too much for it. A little brash. Of course, they're not indigenous, and therefore something of an imposition, don't you think?' William passed him the whisky bottle. 'Breakfast?'

'Thank you,' said Jack. He gulped back a mouthful.

From here on, the next days blurred into each other, punctuated by forays into the high street to the off-licence. There had been an episode when he'd withdrawn money from the bank, he'd become abusive, he knew that, but he couldn't recall the details. Nor did he care. He'd been vaguely aware of people banging on his front door across the square, his mother, his father, Pamela. He let them get on with it. He could do no more than stagger around this park, and the surrounding streets, following William.

Jack was pleased to see his friend again now, looking so changed, and considerably happier.

One afternoon they were, as ever, sleeping it off behind the gardener's hut when there was a sudden thrashing in the undergrowth. Jack and William leapt back against the wall of the hut as four of the hooligans came crashing through. One of them was wielding a baseball bat. Another had a vial of lighter fuel.

8

Pamela sat in Islington police station. It was mid-evening and already the place was heaving with drunks and reckless drivers, and people who'd lost their car radios. She hadn't seen Jack for weeks. No one had. She was shaking, nervous of what she might find.

A man with a bloody nose was brought in, struggling belligerently with two young officers. As they passed, they veered towards her and she jumped back, waking the man slouched beside her. He muttered some mumbled abuse and went back to sleep.

The place smelled awful, a mixture of the basest human odours covered by hourly disinfectant. The floor was strewn with dog ends and half-burnt matches. The desk sergeant looked bored and world-weary, sick of acting as receptionist to the dregs of this city.

Pamela bit the quick in the corner of her thumb nail. A woman next to her coughed like an old dog and she turned her head away in case the woman tried to speak to her again.

'What are you here for, what have the bastards got you here for?' asked the woman. Pamela didn't answer. She could barely speak anyway.

A pair of battered swing doors opened and two dishevelled men, fresh from the cells, were pushed out by a constable. The first was in his fifties and although his face was red and blotchy from years of dedicated wine tasting and there was a graze on his cheek that looked as if he'd fallen over, there was a definitely haughty air about him. He resisted the officer's efforts to hurry him and wore a look of deep offence about the whole business. His hair was matted and his clothes had obviously been donated. The bottoms of his trousers were a good four inches above his battered boots. He was slipping on filthy gloves, with no fingers, as if he were about to take up his box at the opera.

Behind him was a younger man, hovering somewhere between his mid-thirties and an early death in the gutter. His hair was lank and in rats' tails, there was several weeks of growth on his face and he had a similar graze on his cheek as the older man, as if they'd fallen in the gutter together.

The older man guided him past the desk sergeant. The place was somehow beneath them both, though the younger man seemed to care less. He seemed dazed by it all.

'Thank you so much for your hospitality,' the older man was saying.

'Miss?' said the desk sergeant, raising his index finger to Pamela.

'Yes?'

He nodded toward the dishevelled pair. Oh my God, thought Pamela, it's Jack. There seemed to be no sense behind his eyes, the handsome young lawyer looked so wild and furious, and so out of place, that he was unrecognisable to her.

Jack stood in front of her with a cold, hard look in his eyes, waiting for her to 'sort the situation', as if he'd become suddenly used to it. The older man smiled and gave a little bow. He put his hand on Jack's shoulder and led him to Pamela's car outside. They shuffled over in silence. Pamela was at a loss what to say. She'd been shocked to get a phone call from Jack demanding to be picked up at the police station. She'd braced herself for the worst but now that she saw the state that he was in she was shaken to the core.

They walked out to the car. Jack seemed to be silently simmering. He got into the passenger seat after opening the rear door for his companion. Pamela's car, normally smelling only of its plastic seat-coverings and the Magic Tree which swung from the mirror, was overpowered now by the sweet, sickening fumes of stale alcohol. There was an outdoor smell to them as well, cigarettes and bins. Jack had obviously been sleeping rough. It seemed incredible.

She kept her eyes fixed on the road as she drove. Jack and the strange man in the back were silent. Jack was offering no explanation whatsoever. As she pulled up at a traffic light some passers-by glanced in. What an odd situation, a pretty young eighteen-year-old driving tramps around at this time. And he did look, and smell, like a tramp.

'Where've you been, Jack?' she asked. He didn't seem to connect with this and refused to answer. She couldn't even begin to imagine how he'd spent the last six weeks. My God, Jack had even been the duty solicitor at that police station. She tried again.

'How long have you been back?'

Jack slapped his hand on the dashboard. 'Look, I'm sorry I had to call you but I did. I wouldn't've if I'd had any choice but I didn't and so I'm sorry . . .'

Pamela bit her lip. This was an awful thing to see.

'Jack,' she said, 'people have been worried sick. You can't just fuck off for weeks and not tell anyone. You have no right.'

Jack sighed.

'Could you pull over?' he said, coldly.

Pamela pulled over and stopped. They were outside an off-licence. She turned to look at him. His face was still fixed and expressionless, like a man who had rejected everyone and everything for the happy opportunity of an off-licence. He opened the door.

'I don't have any money,' he said. She couldn't believe this. She'd been given no explanation and now he was demanding money from her. She opened her purse and gave him ten pounds.

He turned and looked at her for the first time. There was a terrible dark blackness in his eyes. She gave him another twenty.

She knew that Jack had always had the capacity for something truly vicious within him for revenge. He could commit social murder with words, slay anyone dead with the sharpness of his tongue, but what had been a mannered thing, a convention that they all understood, now was so apparently real. He had gone over the edge. She was frightened of him, but furious and angry with him too. She loved him, but the lovable quality that he'd always had now seemed to be entirely reversed. As if this was the flip side of the coin.

Jack snatched the money away.

'We'll be all right here,' he said, dismissing her. 'Come on, William.' William stirred in the back seat and Jack opened the door and stepped on to the pavement.

'Jack!' screamed Pamela in exasperation. How could he propose just to walk away again? But Jack was already striding toward the brightly lit booze in the window of the off-licence.

The tramp hovered for a moment, almost seemingly embarrassed by Jack's behaviour. It cut Pamela to the quick. William got out of the car and walked to the front window with a vicarage tea party smile on his face.

'I am for ever indebted, madam,' he said to Pamela. 'If ever the opportunity should arise where I can repay you . . .' Pamela was astonished. The man was from another planet, surely.

'William!' screamed Jack's voice from the booze shop door.

'Jack . . .' Pamela whimpered. The old tramp bowed to her. Jack was already in the shop, waving the notes she had given him. There was nothing she could do, he had given her no chance.

William dashed after the tails of his next drink.

At least she could report to Margaret and her mother that he was alive, and in Islington.

As she drove she felt she'd never been so unhappy in all her life. She would have to drive to Margaret's now and there'd most probably be a family summit. Something would have to be done, but they would never believe how low he had sunk. Never. Jack had expressed his sense of tragedy so much better than herself, albeit in a dangerous way.

9

Jack and William returned to the square with their fresh supplies of whisky. Jack had changed since his first day in the park with William. The numbness had gone, the dead look behind his eyes had gone too. Now there was a rage burning inside him. A furious urge to hit out. That was how they'd got themselves arrested. Jack had suddenly retaliated when the teenagers had attacked them and he'd chased them off, into the street, wielding the baseball bat. William had been rather impressed by Jack's sudden effectiveness. Nevertheless he was a little nervous about a possible reprisal.

'Perhaps,' said William, 'in the light of recent events we might be best advised to go to ground for a space.'

'What?'

'Move into that house that you have over there.' William looked up at the sky. 'I fancy we're in for a cold snap.'

'Whatever ... I don't care either way,' said Jack and passed his bottle of whisky to William. William took a warming swig. Even though they had a bottle of whisky each, they were in the convivial habit now of passing the bottle between them. It would be ungentlemanly not to.

Jack had no interest in the house. He walked into the living-room, dropped down, and worked his way through the whisky. He didn't even bother turning on the light.

Jack and William lived in the house in this way for a week or more. Jack never even venturing upstairs. William slept wherever he fell.

Jack woke one morning in crumpled clothes on a dust sheet-covered sofa, his bottle of Scotch sleeping with him, the contents of which had seeped indelibly into the upholstery.

Horrible, hard shafts of light came through the French windows where he'd shattered the panes weeks before. The aluminium trays from the Chinese take-away were scattered across the floor. He had no idea what the time was, or what day. The doorbell was ringing. He ignored it. Just as he'd ignored the cold, and the damp, on the nights he'd slept in the park. He had become expert in shutting out the world. Perhaps it was the afternoon, he thought, he didn't really care.

He focused on the living-room. Maybe, even, he had made one small triumph, he'd managed to reduce the place to even more chaos than Nathaniel, an expert in the field. Nathaniel was part of a former life, a life of ridiculous hope and expectations. Part of the world that ordinary people inhabited. But Jack felt himself to be ordinary no longer. The death of his wife had made him unusual, outside of everyday experience for everyone he knew. Marked out like Cain.

The damn doorbell rang and rang. It began to irritate him. He pulled himself off the sofa. Every bone in his body hurt. His kidneys thudded. He kicked a bottle of Scotch out of his way, and walked across the room. At the dining-room door he stopped. I need a stiffener for this, he thought, and grabbed a half bottle of Chivas from the mantelpiece. William's example had taught him to buy Scotch in half bottles. They fitted so perfectly into one's breast pocket. They were curved expressly for this purpose. He took a swig of it. My God it felt bad but hit the spot so exactly.

He got to the front door and tried to open it. William was on the hallway floor in front of it, wrapped around with a Tibetan rug and copies of the *Evening Standard*. He was sleeping soundly.

'Move, William,' said Jack. William stirred and looked up. A flash of waking annoyance on his face.

'I was here first,' he said. Although he'd slept for some time in this expensive house, the law of the streets had not left him. Inside or outside, it was all the same to him now.

Jack moved him out of the way as the doorbell rang, insistently again. He cracked the front door open on to the harsh light of the day. It was his father.

Michael was wearing a grey trilby and a fine Crombie overcoat.

'Oh my God,' said Jack. 'It's the great psychiatrist making a housecall'.

It was a bitterly cold day, and a rush of freezing air blasted into the hallway. Jack stared at him blankly.

His father stood on the step for a moment, equally expressionless.

'May I come in?' he asked. Jack waved his arm to usher him into the reception room. His father stepped lightly over the trash and mayhem. They had never spoken, why now? Jack flapped at the mantelpiece until he got hold of the half bottle of Scotch.

'Drink?' he said, brandishing the bottle.

'Is that an offer or a challenge?'

'Straight into it, excellent,' said Jack, swigging at the

whisky. 'Do you mind if I tape this conversation and then maybe I can decipher it when you've gone'.

'I haven't much time for this, Jack.'

'When have you ever had time?'

His father's eyes flicked briefly around the room, then he looked directly into his son's bitter eyes. The boy was in a bad way. He was rather shocked to see his own son exhibiting the same signs as the patients that were sent to him on referral.

'You need help, Jack. You're traumatised.'

'Bullshit, I'm pissed,' said Jack.

This was getting them nowhere. They stood for a moment staring at each other like soldiers across a hostile border.

'I can't begin to imagine what you're going through . . .' Michael said.

'Then don't try.'

His father waited for a moment. 'All right, but what about the baby?'

'What about it?'

'She *is* your daughter'.

Jack pulled the Scotch back up to his mouth and took an enormous gulp of it. Like someone doing it as a dare.

'You've never been very good at facing up to your responsibilities . . .'

'Here we go,' said Jack, 'you're such a pompous arsehole.' He'd waited years to say this. Now there was nothing to hold him back. He didn't care what he said to him.

'People pay me a great deal of money to listen to what I have to say.'

Jack's eyes narrowed, and a deep blackness filled them again.

'People pay you money for you to listen, Dad. Forty years and you still haven't learned.'

His father shook his head. 'This is hopeless.' His hat, which he'd held in his hands, as if he wasn't staying anyway, was put back on his head.

'I don't know why you even bothered taking that off,' said Jack.

His father looked away, surveying the debris of his son's house again, shaking his head in disapproval. His son had entirely lost grip. Other people, normal reasonable people, had to deal with tragedies like this, too. Not everyone goes to pieces. But of course his son would, his indulgent son, who could never resist a dramatic gesture. Since he was five years old they had fought. There was still no textbook that could explain it. Standing here, today, in this cold room, he could feel the animosity that had always been there between them as a very real, almost tangible thing.

'Don't worry,' said Jack. 'I'll tell Mother you really tried. You really, really tried this time.'

Michael walked towards the door. He knew what was right for his son, professionally, he knew the sort of help he should have, but he didn't know what to do himself. Defeated and angry he turned to the door.

'You can only be so unpleasant,' he said, '– no matter what you've been through – before people stop caring, Jack, just remember that.'

He shut the door behind him, kicking some of the house's debris into the street.

Jack sunk down on to the sofa again, as William walked into the room looking for the Scotch. Jack passed him the bottle and grabbed the sofa cushions and held them to himself.

The following afternoon was just as cold but William decided to take a walk. Jack was asleep somewhere, he'd finally taken himself upstairs. The boy obviously needed a moment to himself.

William strode across the small park at the centre of the square. The wind was good on his face, and it filled his lungs with it's refreshing coldness, like the ice in a glass of Scotch. Not that William ever took his whisky with ice any more.

It was fine to live in a house for a while but there were so many disadvantages to being locked inside. There was the rather frightening sound of the house as it cooled at night, sudden creaks and groans, which could be horribly disturbing if one happened to be at all delirious at the time. One couldn't just have a pee when one wanted to, first you had to find the particular place for it, or there was merry hell to pay. And there was so much more litter in a house than in one's average public London square. Added to this, one could never be entirely sure what time it was in a house. Outside, a person had the street lamps which never failed to click on and off at dawn and dusk. The clocks in Jack's house had all, somehow, got smashed. Along with the mirrors and the windows. That sort of thing could bring bad luck.

William left the park, for a moment, to look in the skip. Jack and he had been using it as a place to stash the odd bottle.

He pulled the bottle out from beneath a piece of rotting carpet and went to sit with it behind the gardener's green-slatted hut. He rested his back against the old pile of leaves.

Margaret, Michael and Phil let themselves into the house. Margaret had the baby with her. It had been her husband's idea to bring the baby round. When he saw her, Michael believed, he would face up to his responsibilities and snap out of this awful decline.

Margaret wasn't so sure as she walked quietly into Jack's bedroom where he was sleeping, lying in his boxer shorts, face down, with one arm clasping the pillow. Then she put the baby alarm on the bedside table and switched it on. She placed a bottle of baby milk down, and then she gently laid the little baby on the bed beside him.

She looked once more at her son, and at the little child.

Phil had managed, in the mayhem of the kitchen, to make three mugs of tea, and they sat there, silently sipping, watching the baby alarm on the work-top. There was no sound of Jack waking, just the occasional deep sighs of a disturbed sleep.

'I'll just go up and have a look,' said Margaret.

'Stay,' said Michael, firmly. She looked towards Phil for support. Phil stared at the baby alarm.

They heard a little coughing sound from the baby. Then it started to bawl. The baby alarm filled the kitchen with the most terrible yells.

Jack woke suddenly. He opened his eyes and stared into the face of the monstrous thing. It was that nightmare again. He closed his eyes. He opened them again and leapt from the bed, his heart thumping, hyperventilating, he stared at it lying there, making this unearthly, violent, noise.

'My God!' he yelled. He backed away from it, and dashed to the top of the stairs. 'Mum. . .! ? Mum?' he shouted, wavering on the landing, looking down to where he'd fallen on the night she was born.

Downstairs, Margaret looked frantically at Michael and at Phil.

Jack ran back into his bedroom and looked out of the window into the square. It was deserted. He picked up the telephone. 'OK, I get it, we're playing throw the ball to Jack and see if he drops it.'

They could hear him from upstairs on the baby alarm.

'Well it don't work if Jack don't play'.

Margaret put down her mug of tea, but Michael caught her by the arm. The baby was still screaming.

Jack was still listening to the ringing tone of his parents' telephone. It switched to their answer-phone message. They used this answer-phone as a first line of defence, against Michael's clients, against Margaret's selective social life.

'Hello, hello!' he yelled over the message. 'It's me, pick up the phone . . . Come on pick it up. You know if you'd wanted me to call you just had to ring, you didn't have to go this far, you know . . .'

They listened to his voice on the baby alarm as it grew ever more desperate. He might do something irrational, Margaret worried. With Jack it was always possible. Margaret and Phil stood up together, ready to dash up the stairs. Michael sat quietly as if listening to a patient's tape-recorded confessions on a micro-cassette.

'Mum, this is stupid . . .' Jack was saying into the bedside telephone. 'For God's sake, I can't deal with this, I haven't a clue, I'm a mess . . . Mother! Phil . . . Phil's got more sense . . .' He slammed the telephone down and

69

dialled Phil's number. Her phone simply rang and rang. He turned to the baby on the bed.

'Please stop crying, please,' he said to it.

He saw the bottle of milk, which Margaret had left, sitting on the bedside table. He slammed the phone down.

'Hungry, you're hungry. Right then . . .'

He wasn't sure how to pick it up. It seemed like a wriggle of limbs, and its head, the weight of a small medicine ball, had no control whatsoever, and just flopped back over his arm. Its eyes were like marbles that had lost their shine, pieces of glass that you found in the sea, they didn't seem to focus at all. If it was hungry, why wasn't it helping? He knew he was being absurdly irrational, but he was frightened, frightened of this little thing.

Suddenly the baby's mouth formed around the teat of the bottle and the screaming gave way, instantly. He was as shocked by the contented sucking as he had been by its screaming. He held the back of her head with his hand. The bottle popped out of her mouth, and she seemed to stare into his eyes. She seemed to be straining, with every mental effort she could muster, to focus on him. He smiled. He put the bottle back in her mouth, she still held him with her eyes. Her head was warm, her hair fine, like the thread of a bug dangling from an apple tree.

'You've got her eyes, darling. You've got her eyes . . .' he said.

Phil rinsed the mugs out under the kitchen tap, and the three of them quietly let themselves out.

Margaret hovered on the top step, looking back into the house. 'Are you sure about this?' she said.

70

'Of course. You heard him. He's fine,' said Michael.

Margaret turned to Phil. She couldn't make her way down the steps either. 'What if he hurts her when he's drunk?' she said.

Michael was walking into the square.

'He won't. Life goes on. She'll soon show him that.'

10

Jack stared at himself in the bathroom mirror. As he began to shave he saw the bruises all over his body. He pressed them, tentatively, with his finger. He couldn't remember how he'd got any of them. He stared into his eyes and at the dark crescent moons beneath them.

He held the razor under the tap and then he splashed his face with the crisp cold water.

Cleaned up, he walked back into the bedroom and looked into his old school trunk where he'd laid his baby after her feed. She was wrapped snugly up in towels and was gurgling happily. He looked into her eyes and smiled.

If he was actually going to be a father then he was going to have to get himself organised. He called a taxi. Then he picked her out of the suitcase and held her up to his face. There was something absolutely irresistible about her. Her eyes sparkled and she made him feel light-headed. She made him want to protect her.

'So, they've all ganged up on Daddy. Well, that's fine. This isn't so difficult after all, is it?' He held her close so that their noses touched. He giggled. 'It's a piece of piss!'

The baby gurgled back and, as if taking her father's word quite literally, peed all over the clean pair of trousers he'd just put on.

'Oh no . . . stop. . . ! stop. . . !' There was a look of concentration on her face, as a constant stream came his way. He began dashing around the room with her, looking for a shaving mug, or a beer bottle, or anything to catch the constant stream.

The most essential thing right now, thought Jack, is a nappy. But he'd given most of the baby supplies to Pamela. He dashed around the downstairs room, he'd bought so many things over the last months but now he couldn't lay his hands on anything. He was going to have to improvise. He took her downstairs to the kitchen. First of all, he guessed, she was going to need something of a wash. What was it one did with water and babies? He thought back to the classes. He turned on the tap. What you had to do, he remembered, was test the temperature. He held the tip of his elbow under the water. He couldn't help but wonder why it is that one's elbow is so ideally suited to the task.

When the temperature of the water felt reasonable to him he stuck the baby's bum under the tap and gave it a good rinsing. A delighted expression came to her face.

Pleased with his success, Jack set about the business of trying to organise a nappy. He took a clean white hand towel from the drawer. An excellent start. He needed something to absorb the next onslaught, so he found some cotton balls. He wrapped this makeshift nappy around her, as she lay on the draining board. But the final hurdle defeated him. In such a chaotic house as this he didn't stand a chance of finding a safety-pin. He reached into the kitchen drawer for a roll of Sellotape. Perfect.

The baby was still making contented little sounds, and he was rather pleased with his handiwork. The doorbell went and he picked her up to answer it.

There was a middle-aged man in slacks and a Chelsea FC shirt.

'Taxi?' he said.

'Yes, yes, great . . .'

The man's eyes were fixed on the baby and his mouth began to slowly open.

'What's the matter?' asked Jack. The taxi driver shook his head a little, 'Er, nothing, nothing at all . . .'

Jack looked into the baby's eyes. 'You'll freeze if you go out like this . . .' he said cheerily.

'I'll wait in the cab,' said the driver. Odd expression on his face, thought Jack. Had he never seen a man with a baby before?

He dashed back upstairs. He couldn't think what would be the best thing to dress her in. It was a cold day out there, probably an east wind, it might even rain. Certainly not the best weather for new babies. So it'd have to be something practical. He picked up a T-shirt, but the neck hole alone was bigger than the entire width of the baby. It'd just slip off. There was nothing amongst his collection of designer suits and waistcoats that was at all suitable. He ran back downstairs with her. Lying on the worktop was one of the Jiffy bags that they'd packed their framed pictures in. It was new, it was padded and it fitted the baby perfectly when he slipped her in. Just her little face sticking out of the top.

She'd need a hat as well. He saw a half unpacked suitcase and reached in until he found a sock. A fine woollen one with garish stripes running around it.

'It's clean, I promise,' he said as he slipped it on to her head. It was a perfect fit and she looked rather like a little pixie in it.

'You look fab!' said Jack as he gathered her up and took her out to the taxi.

The taxi driver, who, it has to be said, was rather oddly dressed himself, for a man his age, still seemed to be very perplexed about something.

'Where to, mate?' he asked.

'Mothercare!' said Jack. The taxi driver nodded.

Jack dashed into the shop, the baby bobbing in the Jiffy bag in his arms.

'Hello again,' said the assistant on the front desk. 'Thought we hadn't seen you for a while!' Then she saw the baby in the Jiffy bag and caught her breath in shock.

'Yes, hello,' said Jack. 'Look, I've got rather a lot to get . . .'

'Yes. . . ?'

'Can I leave her here with you while I run round?'

'Er, yes, yes . . .' The assistant took the baby in the Jiffy from him, and hovered for a moment, while the other people in the queue stared at the appalling man. The baby seemed to be giggling. Jack began his dash around the shop, filling up one trolley and then another. The manager of the shop wavered in a state of high anxiety as Jack did his rounds. Was a baby wearing a sock on its head, and sitting in an envelope, really the sort of image this branch of Mothercare had taken such pains to cultivate? He looked toward Jack who was test-driving a pram, getting the assistant to test him on an emergency stop.

An hour later the taxi drew up again at Jack's house. The baby was now wearing a dress, and Jack carried her proudly in. The driver, who seemed much encouraged by the improvement, carried in the mountain of baby goods.

It took him four trips.

'Well that's the lot. It has to be. You couldn't have bought anything else,' he said.

'Thanks,' said Jack, picking her up.

'Doesn't she look gorgeous?' he said.

The taxi driver tickled her under the chin. 'Lovely,' he said. 'What's her name?'

Jack looked at the baby closely for a moment and his expression slowly changed. 'Sarah . . .' he said. 'Her name is Sarah.'

Feeding time went rather well, Jack thought. You just had to warm up this milky stuff. It was now mid-evening and he wondered how William was getting on, he hadn't seen him all day. He was probably out there in the square somewhere. It was all for the best. Jack poured the last of the whisky down the sink. Strangely, watching it gurgle away felt better than drinking it.

After her feed Sarah belched. It was so loud that it really quite startled Jack. It delighted him too, she was a real little human being. It was astonishing to Jack that something so young should already have a personality all of her own. She didn't have the best of manners, admittedly, but she was most definitely a person. It was quite incredible to him. She seemed pretty pleased with the effort herself, and they sat together on the sofa for a while watching the Motor Show on the television, Jack explaining to her the intricate niceties of certain engines.

'Do you have a regular bedtime?' he asked her conversationally. 'Or do you just like to hang out and see what comes along? Because, you know, I don't want to be a party-pooper or anything, but it is getting quite late.' She seemed to like the sound of his voice, and her eyes sparkled again. 'Just hang out, eh?' he said.

The telephone rang and he let the answering machine take it. This moment, sitting peacefully with his daughter for the first time, was too precious.

'It's Jack. Chances are my hands are full. Leave a message,' said the answering machine, simply. It was his mother. There was a controlled nervousness in her voice. That over-controlled, over-pleasant voice she used when she was worried, or had to speak her mind. The voice she used when she was 'building up to something'.

'I know you're there, darling, why don't you pick up the phone, sweetheart?'

Jack glanced at the answer-phone. 'Two can play at your game, Mother,' he said, 'can't they?'

His mother was not to be daunted. She'd never officially recognised the limits of answering machine tape.

'Jack,' she continued. 'Phil's terribly anxious to know everything's all right, I've told her not to worry, of course, but you know what she's like.' Jack nearly laughed out loud. His mother was priceless sometimes.

'Maybe you could phone us so we can put her mind at rest. It's only fair, I think you'd agree . . .' His mother's appeals to reason, and fair play, were legendary.

'Nice of her to be so concerned about Phil. Most uncharacteristic,' said Jack.

She cleared her throat, probably in the hope that he would pick the receiver up. '. . . Right, well that's it really, I suppose you must be putting the baby down, it is rather late. Very important to get it into a routine early, dear . . .'

'Thanks for the advice,' said Jack.

His mother hung on the phone for a little longer and then rang off. Jack looked down at little Sarah in his arms. The baby was asleep. Yes, he thought, my mother often has that effect on me too . . .

'What if he's pissed out of his brains in the pub and that poor baby's just lying there in a pile of God Knows What?' said Margaret as she put the phone down.

Michael was rather startled by the sudden change of tone. 'He won't be. Trust me . . .'

This didn't seem to inspire any confidence at all. 'Then trust Jack . . .' he said. This produced a scowl. 'Well, all I can say is that a baby will, most definitely, have the most sobering effect on any man . . .'

Jack sat staring into the baby's face. There were features there, although in miniature still, that were so much of Sarah. Her little cherubic lips were an echo of hers. As the baby slept he stared at her and wept quietly, until he was exhausted.

11

Jack called Nathaniel back. Everything was going surprisingly smoothly. Jack had hired an army of cleaners too and they'd scrubbed and polished every available surface. There was even wallpaper hung in most of the house. Best of all, the first room to be finished was the nursery. There was wallpaper with little pigs on it, all on their way to market. There were mobiles, rather arty ones from Covent Garden, dangling above the lace-bedecked crib, and there was the swearing parrot, sitting well behaved on the windowsill. It was an oasis of optimism within the house. Jack spent hours in there, every evening, staring into Sarah's eyes. He couldn't leave her alone for a moment, it was as if she was part of himself, so much so she almost appeared to share his grief. He felt that it was just the two of them now, against the world. He didn't want to see anyone else, answer any calls, or even telephone West, West & Purnell. He just wanted to stay with his baby.

When the house was finished, it did look truly magnificent. Even Nathaniel's attitude had altered and he now seemed suddenly keen to get the job finished.

On the day that he finally left, Nathaniel hovered on the front step for a moment with a funny little crumpled plastic bag. 'Right,' he said, 'we're done. Bob's men'll finish hanging the hall by this afternoon, and that's it bar the odds and sods.'

'Great' said Jack. This terrible man, who had cost him thousands, and made his life a misery, now seemed incapable of leaving the premises.

Disputes with builders were now such a petty thing, compared to Jack's real experience of life, that it really was nothing to him if he stood there for ever or not. Nathaniel cleared his throat and put his hand into his plastic bag.

'My missus, she um, she knitted these,' he said. He pulled out a pair of pink woollen booties and a rather lopsided cardigan.

'They're beautiful. Thank you, thank you very much,' said Jack, politely. The man was obviously trying to express something. An attempt at compassion, perhaps, but he didn't seem to have the words for it. And it was undoubtedly a new thing for him. He screwed up his plastic bag.

'Well,' he said, 'you've got my number.'

'I certainly have . . .' said Jack.

Jack watched him walk to his Transit van. Nathaniel even turned to wave. It was like watching a character from a former life, or a caricature of someone he once knew.

At three o'clock, Janie, the young health visitor, arrived. Jack knew that the government ran a system of baby spying, that he would be visited sporadically, to see how he was doing. He sat nervously in the nursery while Sarah was weighed in a sort of sling.

'Eleven pounds, six ounces' said Janie.

'That's all right, isn't it?'

'Of course it is, it's a good weight.'

'You mean she's fat?'

'I mean she's fine, she's normal, she's happy. She's healthy.'

Jack shook his head, still worried.

'Maybe I should change her milk?'

Janie smiled.

'I'm not breast-feeding, of course.'

'No, I presumed you weren't.' She laughed. There was something about Jack. She'd enjoyed visiting him. She saw so many babies in a day, but it was refreshing coming here. He wasn't like her other mothers, well, for a start he was a man, but altogether different from the other fathers she encountered too.

All first-time mothers worried themselves silly but he had to be the worst she'd ever met. She was rather attracted to him.

'I'll call again next week and then I won't need to see you . . .' she said to Sarah '. . . until your three-month check. Fat indeed!' She turned to Jack and smiled. He was staring into the crib.

He showed her out and as she walked down the front steps, the door closed behind her, she could hear him dashing back up the stairs to the nursery.

She crossed the square. Two women, arm in arm, were rushing towards her. Then she recognised one of them. It was Margaret, Jack's mother.

'Well, we were just in the area,' said Margaret breathlessly. 'You've been to see the baby? How's she doing, out of interest?'

'Eleven six,' said Janie.

'Oh . . .' said Margaret, nodding her head, surprised and relieved. Contrary to her fears, then, he hadn't let her shrivel away.

81

'Oh . . . um . . . oh' said Phil, equally impressed with the baby's weight.

'Well I'm sure he'll tell you all about it. Are you on your way there now?'

'No,' said Margaret, innocently, as Phil nodded her head in assent. Margaret smiled broadly. 'We thought we ought to let him get on with it . . .'

'Yes . . . let him find his feet . . .'

'I see.'

Margaret cast a glance towards the house. Jack had appeared on the doorstep, going to the dustbin and looking up around the square. 'So!' she said, tugging Phil by the elbow, in case they should be seen. 'We'd better be on our way.'

Phil was still looking earnestly at the health visitor. 'He is putting her down on her back?'

'Yes . . .'

Margaret started to panic. Jack seemed to be searching for something in the square, as if he suspected they were there.

'Of course he is, Phil, now come along, Phil.'

'Wrapping her up properly?' asked Phil.

'Absolutely. Sarah's a very happy little baby.'

Phil's face suddenly drained of blood and she seemed unable to speak anymore.

'Well, I must be off. Bye,' said Janie.

Phil was wavering slightly, and trying to walk away. Margaret held her by the arm

'Phil . . .' she said.

Phil was almost in tears, but smiling bravely. 'I'm fine, honestly. It's lovely that he's named her . . . I just hadn't expected it, that's all. It's a shock, that's all.' Her face was quivering.

In some ways they'd all thrown themselves so much into the drama of the new baby, and Jack's crisis, that they'd failed to give time to proper grief. Perhaps it was for the best, the way it should be.

Margaret looked back at the house. Jack had gone. She put her arm around Phil. They were such different sorts of women. Even though they were the same age, Phil had lived the last eighteen years without a man. She wore her hair straight, sported capes, and lived in an odd two-bedroomed flat in Labroke Grove. She involved herself in blatantly left-wing causes. All this, Margaret felt, had made her rather hard and unapproachable, but now she looked so suddenly distraught and vulnerable.

The baby alarm woke Jack in the night. Sarah was crying, a plaintive, exhausted sort of crying, as if the child were not just uncomfortable, but unhappy too.

He went into the nursery and spoke to her softly. He picked her out of the cot, but there was nothing he could do to console her. He carried her down the stairs to the living-room. Holding her in his arms he reached for a tape cassette and slipped it into the stereo. The stack system lit up and the opening strains of Simply Red's 'Stars' filled the room; the track that he and Sarah had danced to on that last day in the old house in Hammersmith. A song they'd danced to so many times.

Jack began shuffling slowly around the room with the baby Sarah in his arms. The red and green lights of the stereo system, and the moonlight, gave a soft, calming light to the room. Jack let the lyrics play through his head. The baby had stopped crying, but the tears were streaming down his face now. Everything still seemed so unreal, and so impossible to understand, that it overwhelmed him entirely.

It was again the early hours of the morning when the phone rang from University College Hospital. Margaret pulled Michael out of bed.

'Come on,' she said, 'we're needed.' She didn't trouble with make-up, or even combing her hair but just threw on a one-piece frock and a mackintosh.

They found their way through the maze of the hospital, quieter tonight than before. They'd phoned Phil and she was on her way too. It was a good hospital, but such a desperate place in the middle of the night. It was also an intensely painful place for them all to have to return to.

Margaret went straight to the reception desk, with a look of hardened determination on her face.

'Excuse me . . .' she said, but as she spoke she heard the sound of footsteps coming towards her along the corridor. There was a young, tired, doctor, with Jack beside him, Sarah in his arms. Margaret and Michael rushed up to him. Phil was making her way towards them.

'Jack, Jack, whatever's the matter?' cried Margaret.

'What's happened?' asked Phil, behind them.

Jack looked at the floor, he tried to smile, but failed.

The young doctor held Margaret by the forearm. 'She has wind,' he said, flatly. Jack looked up at the doctor, hurt in his eyes.

'Very bad wind' said the doctor, correcting himself.

Margaret grabbed her son, and took him in her arms, almost weeping. 'Oh Jack, you stupid boy.'

'She couldn't breathe . . .' said Jack, almost sobbing, 'she was crying.'

'Of course she was,' said Margaret and took the baby from him. 'Hello, darling.' The baby looked tired, but fine. There was a thin, pathetic, smile on her face. She did look so much like Jack.

Jack turned to the doctor. 'I'm sorry' he said, weakly.

'No problem. Goodbye.'

They began the walk to the car park.

'You are a fool' said Phil. 'We do know how well she's doing . . . how well you're doing.'

'I feel so stupid' said Jack.

His father sniggered. 'Don't. Your mother rushed you into hospital in the middle of the night when you were only a week old – a cold, a bad cold, but only a cold.'

'Where's your car?' asked Margaret.

Jack bit his lip. 'I didn't come by car.' The three of them stared at him.

'I called an ambulance . . .'

12

It was early evening and there was a sharp, precise, ring on the doorbell. Jack went to open it with Sarah in his arms.

It was William. Jack hadn't seen his friend for several weeks. He guessed that William had seen all the building activity going on and had retreated again into the park. But now that the builders had gone he found it safe to approach the house again.

William was wearing his ridiculous fur-lined hat, with the Labrador ears, and looked rather the worse for drink. One of his shoes appeared to have come apart at the toes and he'd wrapped a bit of rag around it. He was wearing a light tweed overcoat several sizes too small for him and he was smiling broadly. His eyes lit up to see the baby.

'So the rumours circulating the park are true!' he said. 'The little princess has come home. My heartiest congratulations, and most sincere felicitations, Jack.'

Jack smiled. 'Thankyou, William'.

'You look well. Better, much better like this.' Jack could barely believe that just a short time before he had looked something like William did now. William craned his head to look past Jack into the warmth and the comfort of the newly decorated hallway.

'The old place is looking good too,' said William, nodding in approval.

'Yes, it's almost finished.'

'Oh, well, plenty of time.'

The two men stood, simply staring at each other for several moments. William took another step up towards the house, and waited for a gesture from Jack. Jack moved slightly, to the centre of the doorway. William cleared his throat.

'I thought perhaps I might take the baby out for a little walk, just around the park . . .' he said.

Jack let out a short, involuntary, laugh, and looked at his old comrade with an incredulous expression of horror on his face.

'William, I, . . . that's just not possible. You know I can't let you do that.'

William said nothing, but a slight frown spread across his forehead. A frown that had a whole history of disappointments such as this behind it. Jack dug his hand into his pocket and pulled out a couple of ten-pound notes.

'Look, here, take this'.

William stared, in disbelief, at the money. He was so offended he couldn't speak. He turned on the step and strode off across the road, back to the undergrowth of the park.

'William . . . William!'

Jack closed his front door and leaned against it. Why had he offered him money?

'Shit!' he shouted in fury. He walked back into the dining-room. The house looked so perfect, every surface gleaming. Arty pots, flamboyant lamps, designer comfort everywhere. This house expressed as little of his true inner feelings as ever it did William's, but their two worlds could never meet here again.

Later that evening the doorbell rang a second time. It was Pamela, with a bottle of wine. She'd obviously had a few drinks already. He guided her into the kitchen and opened the bottle. They sat for an hour, gulping down the first bottle, and then another. She bore so many resemblances to her sister, but at the moment there was an emptiness at the heart of her, which Sarah had never had.

'I'm such a miserable cow really,' she said. 'When I haven't got something I want I'm unhappy and then when I get it I always think of a reason why I don't really want it, and I'm unhappy again.'

'But that's just silly,' said Jack. 'You've been looking forward to this, ever since I've known you. You've talked about practically nothing else.'

'It'll just be three years of putting my life on hold.'

'You're going to university, not prison.'

Pamela tried to smile. 'If I was going to go I should have gone last year. I've just wasted the whole year, and now I've still got the whole of the summer to waste. I just let everything slip away.' It was kind of Jack to be trying to encourage her, to cheer her up, considering his own circumstances. All her expectations of life now seemed to be altered.

'I just want to get on with things now, that's all,' she said.

'Don't wish your life away. God alone knows, it's short enough.' What would have, ordinarily, been perhaps a bit of a cliché, hung in the air, as they gulped at the wine in silence. There was a comfort in the silence too. Right since the very moment of Sarah's death there had been no pressure on either of them to come out with any platitudes. No need to behave in the way that Margaret felt she had to, however nobly, or to withdraw into some sort of anonymous professionalism like Michael. They were the closest in this tragedy, they were its contemporaries.

'Listen,' said Jack, 'I haven't worked out what to do with her clothes and things. I'd really like you to have some stuff if you want it.'

Perhaps it was that awful word 'stuff', but Pamela's eyes began to fill with tears.

'Don't get upset . . . you'll start me off.'

'I have to go,' she said. 'You will let your mum and Phil know how things are going, won't you?'

'Are you sure they didn't send you?'

'They need you to need them, Jack.'

'I will soon. I promise. It was really nice seeing you, really nice.'

'And you.'

They hugged. They hugged for perhaps a little longer than they should have done. Then they kissed.

'I think I should go,' said Pamela, abruptly.

'Yes, yes, maybe . . .' said Jack.

After she had gone Jack sat for a while, staring into the darkness of the garden beyond the French windows. It was so very difficult to keep a level head. He seemed to be veering from one crisis to another: he'd offended William, he'd practically been in a clinch with Pamela. He was losing his centre of control.

There was a dark, eerie, shape swaying in the garden outside, like a kind of phantom, tugging at him. It frightened him, even though he knew it was merely an old, straggling, lilac tree, that needed lopping back.

He began working out a plan to normalise his life, even if it was only filling it up with activity, or else he knew he'd screw things up entirely. End up in the park with William.

He'd do the decent thing. He'd invite Margaret, Michael and Phil to Sunday lunch, he'd let them have their visiting rights. And on Monday he'd return to work at West, West & Purnell.

Jack went to sleep a little more at peace with himself.

He telephoned his mother.

'What's the matter? What's happened, now just don't panic at all, darling, your father and I will be straight round. We were just going out. It's bridge, of course, but we'll cancel. Thank God you caught us in time . . .'

'. . . Nothing's the matter, Mum. There's nothing wrong.'

'Just calm down,' said Margaret, 'we'll be right there.' Jack began to giggle. He could hear his mother putting her hand over the phone and calling to Michael. 'He's hysterical, we've got to get over to Jack's.'

'Mum! Mum!' yelled Jack.

'Just calm down! Take deep breaths,' Margaret yelled back, while gesticulating to Michael to grab their coats.

'Oh, this is ridiculous, I wish I hadn't called. I knew I shouldn't have bothered,' snapped Jack.

Margaret went suddenly quiet. 'You're such a silly bitch sometimes.'

'Jack, there's no need for . . .' Margaret searched for words.

'I'm phoning up to invite you to Sunday lunch . . .'

Now she was truly silenced. 'Oh . . . oh, I see, on Sunday?' she said.

'Well, obviously.'

Michael had grabbed his car keys and was struggling to put his coat on. Margaret turned to him, a smile on her face.

'Just a moment, darling . . .' she said into the phone. 'Michael, it's Jack. He's inviting us to Sunday lunch. Are we doing anything this Sunday?'

Michael stared at her for a moment and then he began shaking his head slowly from side to side. She knew they weren't doing anything.

'Yes, we'd love to, darling,' she said, after a pause, as if they'd had to discuss it. 'Shall we say one o'clock?'

'Yes, one o'clock would be perfect.'

'So we shall see you then.'

'Yes.'

'Would you like us to bring anything?'

'No, perhaps just a bottle of something.'

'Yes, perfect. We've just had another of those cases from Michael's wine club. Of course, I don't mean we'll bring the whole box, just something nice, we don't want to get too boozy, do we?'

'No, of course not.'

'What are you planning to cook? A roast?'

Jack really didn't want this to get too involved. 'I haven't thought yet,' he said.

'Ah, good, because we've a wonderful little butcher who lets me have very good roasting beef. Better than you'd find in N1, I'm sure, so shall we say I'll pop round at eleven and it'll be perfect for lunch at one, won't it? So that's settled then.'

Jack sighed. It was pointless to try to oppose her when she had something set in her mind.

'I thought I'd invite Phil as well,' he said. Best to get it on the table now, as it were.

'Oh, Phil, right, right. Yes, I suppose you have to,' she said, as magnanimously as she could.

Jack shook his head.

Michael had already poured himself a whisky.

'It'll mean a bigger piece of beef, but no matter. I don't think she feeds herself, unless she's out. So there we are then. Have you telephoned her yet?'

'No, no, I called you first,' said Jack. The smile returned to Margaret's face. She couldn't help but be so jealous of her son's attentions. When Jack put the phone down he poured himself a whisky.

He felt he'd earned it.

Margaret arrived at ten-thirty, not eleven as threatened, and Jack was still in his dressing-gown. She laid her handbag on the hall table and kissed him on the cheek. Jack looked into the street where his father was struggling out of the car with a huge cardboard box.

'Hi,' said Jack as he came through the door.

'Hi . . .' said his father. Repeating the expression rather fatuously, as if it were no sort of greeting between father and son.

'Just put the veg and everything in the kitchen,' said Margaret, 'and I'll get set-to just as soon as you've got the other bits and pieces in. Now where's my little girl?' Jack led them downstairs to the kitchen room. Margaret picked Sarah up.

'Does she look a little peaky to you?' she said.

'Wind,' said Jack.

Michael came in with a second cardboard box filled with saucepans, a roasting tin, and a gravy boat.

'You know how I like to work with my own things,' said Margaret, 'and I wasn't sure whether you'd managed to get around to a gravy boat yet.' She began to bounce the baby up and down, and coo at her in a rather shrill voice.

'We've had three gravy boats for years,' said Jack.

Michael dumped the box down and glanced at his son. There was a sort of world weariness on his face which said 'just let her get on with it'.

'Would you like a drink, Dad?' said Jack.

'Yes, good idea.'

'Yes, I'll pop the kettle on,' said Margaret, 'can you do that for me, Jack?' The logic of this defeated him.

The doorbell rang. Margaret looked sharply at her son. What sort of intrusion was this?

Jack went to the door. There was Phil, wrapped up in one of her capes. She looked at him sheepishly.

'Ah, hello, Jack. I'm early, I know, but I wondered if you needed anything getting, any help in the kitchen?' said Phil.

'Yes, yes,' said Jack, 'I need all the help I can get in the kitchen.' There was a withering look on his face. He led her through the hallway.

'And where's our little girl?' she said, quickly brightening at the prospect of seeing her granddaughter.

As they turned into the kitchen the two women stared at each other.

'Already here!' said Phil.

'Yes, we are,' said Margaret quietly.

'Shall I take you for a spin round the house now it's all done, Dad?' said Jack.

They went into the dining-room, where his father stood for a while in silence staring at the wall.

'I'm surprised you didn't have that knocked through,' said his father.

93

'Mm. Would have meant losing the room above, of course, it's a structural wall, but I'm sure you're right.'

The rest of the tour was conducted without conversation. Every now and then his father's eyes picked out odd little splashes of errant paintwork that Jack hadn't noticed until now. Michael rolled the balls of his feet back and forward every time he hit the smallest creak in a floorboard.

He looked out of the second floor landing window down into the garden, which hadn't been tackled yet.

'If you're going to plant fruit trees, you need to do it now, to get the benefit of them,' he said.

'Right, right, of course . . .' Perhaps a nice little orange grove and some pomegranates, Jack was tempted to say.

Eventually, when he couldn't bear to drag the tour out any longer he returned his father to the kitchen room.

'Interesting way of peeling potatoes . . .' Margaret was saying as she looked over Phil's shoulder at the sink. She was holding Sarah with one arm while she mixed batter for Yorkshires with the other.

Jack sat on the sofa. His father had picked up the Sunday papers from the hallway and was looking at the sports pages. Jack wondered why it was that if he was so interested, they'd never been to any sort of match together.

It was all going terribly well.

'You don't find this beef too bloody?' said Margaret, over lunch.

'No, no, not at all, it's absolutely perfect' said Phil.

'Horse-radish?' asked Margaret.

'Thankyou, I have some.'

'Have I given you enough Yorkshire?'

'Quite enough, thank you, Margaret.'

Jack was a little quiet. How different this silently strained scene was from the lunch parties they'd had in the old house in Hammersmith. Though the beef was quite succulent the sound of interminable chewing was unbearable. So Jack decided to make his announcement that this was a 'celebration', that tomorrow he was going back to work. Smiles broke out for the first time, and during the hearty good wishes that followed he was even able to pour himself another glass of wine without being checked. They were genuinely pleased. He was getting himself back together at last. The only part they didn't agree with, naturally, was his avowed intention to take baby Sarah to work as well.

After lunch the table was cleared with frightening efficiency, the women carrying the things out, and overseeing Michael as he stacked the dishwasher.

Then Margaret decided that it was time for Sarah's nappy to be changed.

'Yes,' said Jack, reaching for a nappy, and walking over to his daughter. 'Come here, sweetheart.'

'Oh, let me,' said Phil, 'you relax with your father.' Jack raised his eyebrows.

'No, I'll do it,' said Margaret. 'I'll be quicker.' Jack withdrew as the two women set about the task together. There followed a considerable amount of fumbling and comments about how 'impractical' these new types of nappies were, but eventually the thing was done. Margaret then began trying to bend Sarah's arm, at every place but the elbow, to get it into a vest. Jack felt a little stab of pain for her.

'I think you're being a bit rough with her, Mum,' he said.

'Nonsense. Babies are more resilient than you think.' She wrenched the vest on. 'There we are,' she said, triumphantly. As Jack walked over to take his daughter, Margaret swept past him. He went to pick up the clothes that the two women had discarded, but Phil gathered them up before he had a chance. Gritting his teeth he sat down again, battling bravely to remain polite. He was determined to resist causing a scene.

Margaret was touring the room with Sarah. Every time she passed Phil the other woman seemed to expect Margaret to hand the baby to her, for a 'turn', but she didn't. Jack felt that his daughter had been suddenly stolen from him.

'And where d'you intend keeping her at the office? In a filing cabinet?' asked Margaret, brusquely.

'That's a good idea,' he said. Phil had found the laundry basket and was busying herself by hanging the little clothes on the radiator.

'This isn't a joke. She's not a doll,' said Margaret.

'I'd be very happy to have her, Jack,' said Phil.

'Oh don't be silly, Phil,' said Margaret. 'You were a shambles as a mother, you said so yourself. And anyway a lot's happened to you, dear. You're still grieving. We'll have her.'

There was a terrible silence, as both women glanced at Jack. They probably meant well, he thought, but he couldn't bear it.

'I don't want to leave her with anyone at the moment.'

Margaret was deeply shocked. 'We're hardly anyone!'

'I have to cope on my own.'

His father looked up for once. 'He's right,' said Michael.

'No he isn't,' said Margaret, rounding on him. She

turned to Jack. 'You've got us. You should rely on us.'

'I want her at work with me and if I can't I'm not going back. It's as simple as that. For now.' He was determined to stand his ground.

'Well, when the novelty's worn off give us a call and let's hope we're free.' Margaret turned to look at Phil. 'I think she'll finish her feed now,' she said and handed her to Phil. 'There you are, Phil. You do the honours.'

'But you needn't worry,' he said, 'I'm going to get a nanny.'

Margaret and Phil looked directly at each other, this was an absolute bombshell to them. They both turned to stare at Jack open-mouthed.

'A nanny!' they said in unison.

13

Jack was dressing for work. He was a little nervous of his first day back. He pulled out a plain tie and a new white shirt he'd never worn. His hand fell on his favourite Jasper Conran suit. Then he put it back in the wardrobe. It was black. The last thing he wanted to appear was at all funereal, it was going to be a difficult enough day for everyone anyway. People wouldn't really know what to say to him, he knew that. He didn't want to spend the entire working day receiving condolences. He wanted to avoid them as much as everybody else. He chose a smart suit and a lively silk tie. He set off for work.

He hadn't experienced the rush hour for a while and it was rather a shock. The lemmings of London clattered around him, swinging their briefcases, fondling their mobile phones, all of them with a look of lateness on their faces, and the uniform grey visage of dread.

As Jack bobbed through Finsbury Circus, people turned to stare at him as he passed. Like them he had a briefcase at his side, but unlike them he was wearing a rucksack, with all Sarah's things crammed in. And strapped to his chest, in a sort of papoose, Sarah was sleeping happily. The rush hour was nothing to her. She seemed to enjoy the gentle jogging of his steps.

He turned into the foyer of West, West & Purnell, and

threw a cheery 'good morning' to the doorman. It was all going well.

The lift doors were just closing but he managed to catch it with his foot. The doors slid open again. The mirrored walls of the lift interior presented him with three Annas, all of them looking momentarily non-plussed. But she smiled.

It was good to see him back.

He smiled broadly and they stood next to each other. Anna took a lingering look at his ruck sack and raised her eyebrows.

'Taken up fell walking?' she asked, breaking the ice.

'You'd be amazed how much crap one of these things needs.' Anna leaned around to look at the baby's face, now awake to the excitement of the movement of the lift.

'She's sweet. Sarah's eyes.'

'Yeah.'

Jack was impressed. Her cynical humour and her direct approach to the problem in hand could sometimes actually be quite warm. It was certainly refreshing. Anna looked at him and smiled. Then she said: 'I don't want the whole place disrupted, Jack. I know things are difficult for you but unfortunately that holds no sway within these walls. This is a law firm not a nursery. You have an obligation to the other partners.'

This was still preferable to sympathy, he told himself. He preferred her to be herself. You knew where you stood.

'You won't even know she's here, I promise,' he said, and stepped out of the lift into the large open plan reception area. He walked across the monogrammed pile, as Anna arrived at her office door. Suddenly the receptionist had abandoned her swivel chair. His secretary, Jackie, had appeared. The typing pool were here in force. Even Mervyn, the mail boy, had stopped with his trolley. All of them cooing over little Sarah, doe-eyed and abandoning the English language. People had appeared from everywhere to gather around him. He was being mobbed.

Jack turned towards Anna's office door. She was standing there, four-square, surveying the scene, her face growing gradually more severe.

Jack smiled uneasily as he caught her eye. He nipped swiftly into his office.

He had been a partner here for five years and he knew he'd have a great deal to catch up on after his time away. Cases that he'd been working on when Sarah had died were now referred to other people. Some, miraculously, had even been settled. Anna had decided that it would be the best thing if he spent his first morning back wading through a pile of monotonous notes on cases pending. Boring, but necessary. Or 'BBN' as Jackie, had come to call these tasks over the years. He ploughed through the interminable notes on disputes over intricate parts of machinery that finally produced God knows what but had substantially fucked up a new office building in W1, costing, potentially, millions. After his experience of Nathaniel, cases such as this rather appealed. He searched vainly for something that might serve to give him a measure of entertainment. A paternity suit against a cabinet minister would be nice, but these were the sorts of hoaxes any company like this got every day. There was a damn fine oil slick case, in which countless innocent seals and seabirds had been scrubbed down by the RSPCA, but their clients were registered in Liberia, and were responsible for the slick.

After an hour of this Jack took himself to the mezzanine floor where the coffee machine and a small kitchen for employees were housed. He made himself a coffee and boiled a kettle to heat up Sarah's mid-morning feed. His friend Rob came in. They looked at each other for a few moments, then Rob clasped him affectionately by the arm. Rob had called and called after Sarah's death and then finally given up, knowing that Jack needed to face people again in his own time.

'How's it going?' asked Rob, pleased to see him back, but not knowing quite what to say. 'I see you've already got a pile of stuff on your desk,' he said, smiling broadly.

'It's fine,' said Jack, 'though God knows what I've read this morning. I think I'm just scanning the pages. It all seems so petty, somehow.' Rob took his arm affectionately. 'Yeah, I'm sure it must do. You can always join me in Divorce, of course, then you'll know what real pettiness is. You know, this morning I've had a seventy-six-year-old on the phone. Married fifty-four years, five children, twelve grandchildren. Wants a divorce because he thinks it's time for a change. Doesn't want to loose custody of the dog, though. It'd drive you mad.'

'Yeah, I don't imagine I'd have much patience for that right now.'

'Well you just keep your head down and take it easy, as they say,' said Rob.

Sally, one of the junior partners, came in carrying her own mug. Sally was one of the more vivacious of the younger women, tending to stun the young male partners at Law Society balls with gowns that seemed to be made of foil and held together with pins.

'Jack, how are you?' she said, stroking his arm and kissing him on the cheek.

'Sally, I'm fine, fine.'

'It's good to see you back.'

'Thank you.'

'And where's the baby?'

'She's up in the office with Jackie and the girls.'

'Oh great, I've not seen her yet. Listen if you need any help . . .'

'Thanks.'

'I don't mean just at work. I mean at home, you know, baby-sitting or anything, just call.'

'I will.' Sally kissed him again and walked away. Her coffee mug was still sitting on the draining board.

Rob shook his head slowly from side to side. 'Unbelievable' he said, as he watched Sally glide to the lift. 'I don't believe it, they're all over you.'

'Don't be daft, it's the baby. They're all over the baby.'

'Yeah, but the baby comes with you and to have the baby they'll have you too.'

'I don't know what it is. You should have seen the looks I got in Finsbury Circus this morning. All the men just ignored me, except for those that gave me the sort of look that suggested I was letting the side down. But the women, they smiled, all of them. Well, most of them, anyway. And that's against Rush Hour Rules.'

'I'll tell you what it is. It's pulling power, matey. That's what it is.'

Now it was Jack's turn to shake his head. He'd always felt uneasy with the male bonhomie of the office. He returned to his pile of papers.

Anna sat in her office, trying to concentrate her mind on the company's mid-term review. All she could hear was the screaming of a baby in the outer office. She glared

102

through the glass of her office door. Jackie was pacing up and down with it. She disliked writing reports and every time she managed to get the thing to flow naturally, so the baby screamed again, and she lost it.

Jackie came into Jack's office, a little distraught, clutching a screaming baby to her bosom.

'She won't settle. I think she's overtired by it all.'

Jack put his hand over the telephone receiver. He was taking a call from the company lawyer of a City institution. 'She'll go off if you take her in the car,' he said. 'She like's the movement.'

'I can't, and no one else is free out here.'

Jack thought for a moment . . .

Things seemed to have quietened and Anna began on her speech to the board. Thank God Jack had managed to do something. He'd given her his express undertaking that the baby would be invisible while it was within the building. Then she saw Mervyn, the mail boy, pass by her door. Was that a baby in the mail trolley, sleeping soundly, among the briefs? The place was falling to pieces.

By lunchtime, as he'd expected, he was weary of people's heads suddenly jolting around his office door, asking how he was. The sympathy in their eyes was exhausting. It was hard work putting them at their ease. Most of these encounters were to make them feel better, not him, he thought. They were getting it all out of the way at the start. He much preferred to deal with people on less-than-equal terms, i.e. bullying them about something.

He decided to take Sarah for lunch at his favourite little Italian restaurant hidden away in a cobbled yard. It was where Sarah and he had conducted the opening scenes of their life together, eating pizzas and drinking Chianti, always sitting at 'their' table. He walked up to the door. Where had it gone? Luigi's Pizzeria, a snug little place, with warm pink tablecloths and bottles hanging in straw, had disappeared. In its stead was a rather trendy French brasserie, with metal-topped tables.

He walked in with his baby. They'd got a new wooden floor that looked as if it'd been plundered from a fine old warehouse, stripped and sanded, and botched into here. The bar was in a different place, running all down one side of the brasserie with Pernod and Mexican beer doubled up against a mirrored backdrop.

The tables were strewn with yellow plastic ashtrays that could only be considered stylish because they bore the name Ricard. He preferred the old foil things that Luigi took such pride in changing between courses.

Sitting just this side of the bar was a dashing young Frenchman, obviously the new owner because he had a glass of white wine in one hand and a calculator in the other. Jack didn't like owners who sat with the diners. The young man was very well dressed too – if one is impressed by every article of a person's clothing having someone else's name on it. In this case: the T-shirt Moschino; the shoes Cardin; the belt YSL.

The walls had been covered with intimations of France: Metro signs, Gauloise advertisements, line drawings of shallots. The menu was hand-written in a sort of amateur calligraphy, with photocopied 'specials' paper-clipped to them. The French onion soup advertised itself as 'coming with croutons'. As if it wouldn't anyway. It was the sort of menu designed to speak clearly to idiots and tourists used only to overpriced burger joints. Not to people who liked to discover a little tucked-away place and make it one of their regular haunts, develop some affection for it.

The only other diners in the place exemplified the former sort of coterie perfectly. Four young guys, hungry City oafs, in shiny suits and white socks, their hair slicked down. As they downed their Heineken, they grew louder and louder, and hit each other around the face with the plastic heat-sealed menus.

In the window, two other men talked heatedly about the problems faced by independent television companies in the face of Network Centre. They were drinking Perrier, but were equally as noisy as the younger men. Naturally they presumed their conversation was of interest to all. It was a London Lunch.

He reminded himself that he'd come here to relax, and show the place to Sarah. Luigi would have spoiled her terribly.

Jack took a seat at the back of the restaurant approximately where the old table would have been. He settled Sarah, in a carry-seat, on the chair next to him, and opened one of the files that had taken his interest. The waitress came over.

'Isn't he beautiful? How old?' Jack looked up, the waitress was American, with a broad, friendly smile and she was already tickling Sarah under the chin.

'She's three months,' he said.

The young woman was blonde, with stunning blue eyes, and she wore a long white apron over a short black skirt, a black waistcoat, and monkey boots with ankle socks. Probably a student taking a year out, thought Jack, travelling to see the world by working in restaurants. A French restaurant in London, an Italian in Paris, a Chinese in Rome, he imagined.

'Is he yours?' she asked.

'No, I stole her.' God, it was refreshing to trot out stupid answers to simple questions after the strain of the morning.

The waitress's face froze for a moment, as Americans do when they're subjected to British humour. Then she smiled, and pulled out her pencil.

'OK, dumb question. What'll it be?' Jack looked at the pretensions on the menu.

'Um, I'd like a hamburger, rare, with whatever it comes with.'

'Anything to drink?'

Jack could have murdered a pint of beer, or a bottle of Chianti.

'Coffee. Cappuccino,' he said. She smiled at the baby again. She seemed to be really taken with her. Jack was proud. He liked anyone who like his baby.

'And what about gorgeous? Anything for him?'

It was odd, thought Jack, that because he was a man alone with a baby she naturally presumed it was a boy.

'No he's . . . fine,' he said. 'I've got something for her'. He produced a little plastic pot, three quarters full of mushed-up apricot pudding. The waitress stared at it as if it were radioactive.

'D'you want me to warm it up?'

'Um, yes. Thank you. That would be nice. She prefers it warm.' She smiled incredulously. Did it make that much difference to mush?

'I made it myself,' said Jack, proudly.

'I bet you did,' she said. He liked her manner.

Jack turned back to his file.

The city lads, in their shiny suits, were getting louder, and Jack looked up to glare at them, it was disturbing

Sarah. Although he'd fancied a drink himself, he hated lunchtime drinking. There was always something abusive, and cheap, about people who drank in London at lunchtime. Fine in Rome, in a piazza, or in Paris by the Seine, but somehow Londoners just couldn't handle it at all. They got loud and foolish every time. And wasted the afternoon.

The waitress walked over to them with another tray of beer. As she got to the table, the loudest of the guys reached out his hand and touched the back of her knee.

'Please don't do that,' she said. She laid the tray on their table and began portioning out the bottles. Then the guy's hand went to the back of her leg again. He ran his palm, quite roughly, up her thigh. She pushed a beer towards him, smiling this time, and then when he was sufficiently off guard she whacked it into his lap.

'Bitch!' he yelled, jumping up. She looked at him coldly.

'Gee, I'm sorry.'

'What did you do that for?'

'It was an accident.'

'Like fuck it was.'

The owner laid his calculator aside and marched over to the table, glaring at the waitress.

'What's going on?' he said. His accent was French. Genuine French, but in a rather forced and public way, like the decor of the brasserie.

'Amy, get the gentleman a cloth.' She stood for a moment, surely he knew she was innocent. 'Now!' he bawled at her. 'And get the gentleman another beer.'

'Oh, God . . .' the lout was muttering, 'I'll go back to the office smelling of beer now.'

Jack smiled. It served the dickhead right.

As Amy passed Jack's table she caught his eye, a look of mock regret playing on her face. 'Silly, silly, me,' she said.

She took her time about the guy's beer. Bringing Jack's lunch first.

'Here we are,' she said, brightly. 'One hamburger, rare, one cappuccino and . . .' She stared at the plastic pot '. . . one goo.'

'Thanks.'

She went over to the lads, delivered the beer, and as she turned away Jack saw her jump. She closed her eyes and counted to five. He was appalled. The guy had pinched her backside. There was a moment of tension in the air, then she came over to Jack. He held her with his eyes for a moment. She was breathing quickly, and although she was controlling it admirably, there was a dark black fury in her eyes. She must really need this job, thought Jack.

'Here, let me do that,' she said, reaching for the baby food, and instantly lightening up.

'Aren't you busy?'

'I'll be OK for ten minutes.' She picked up Sarah. 'Come on you. What's his name?'

She was being kind. He didn't want to embarrass her.

'Um . . . John,' he said. 'His name's John.'

Amy took 'him' to the back of the restaurant and Jack returned to his work and his burger. As Amy passed the Frenchman he stared at her cynically. 'Getting broody, Amy?' he asked.

'If I was, you'd be the last to know.'

Jack was enjoying himself. It was quite a little soap opera. The sort of lunch that could easily be followed by a lawsuit. Well, in America, at least. The burger hadn't been half bad either.

When he'd finished lunch Amy came back over with Sarah.

'How're you doin'?' she said. Sarah looked perfectly happy in her care. Baby and waitress were cooing at each other.

'Great, that was great, thank you very much.' He was enjoying being polite and charming to her now. It seemed the radical thing to be in this restaurant today.

'Here, I washed his bowl and the bottle.'

'Thank you'.

'He's a gorgeous baby.'

'Yes, I think so too.'

'Anything else?'

'Just the bill, thanks.' He took Sarah in his arms. Amy went over to the owner.

'Bill for number three, Alain, please,' she said. He swung slowly round on his zinc-topped barstool. 'And seven?' he said, coolly.

'They've not finished yet.'

'Then where are they, *chérie*?' he said. Amy looked to where the two smart media types had been sitting. They'd done a runner.

'Oh shit,' she said. She ran to the front of the restaurant, looking out into the street. Then she ran into the yard.

Alain printed out Jack's bill and brought it to his table. Jack didn't like this guy at all. The Frenchman laid Jack's bill on the table without speaking, looking into the yard, where Amy stood, confused and frustrated. He was smiling. In some perverse way he was enjoying his waitress's discomfort. It was bizarre. Weird.

Amy walked slowly back in.

'How much do I owe?' she said, resigned to her fate. Alain went over to the till.

'Thirty-seven pounds and fifty pence,' he said, adding sharply, 'not including service.'

'Tell me, Alain. Did you see them leave?'

He didn't respond. 'Coffees for table four please, Miss Fletcher,' he said, as if he was sending her back to the City lads as a further punishment. She was obviously boiling inside, but a word now would mean disaster for her. Jack was getting angry too. Amy went into the kitchen for the coffee.

Jack held his credit card out to the owner. 'I'll pay the other bill as well,' he said.

'Were they friends of yours?' Alain asked.

Jack disliked the supercilious tone in his voice. His eyes grew dark. 'Why don't you just shut it and take the money?' he said.

The two men stared at each other like two stags on a ridge.

'Certainly. It makes no difference to me.'

'I'm sure it doesn't,' said Jack. The moral victory was his. This man really was without any feeling at all, except, perhaps, for the money in his cash till. Jack began packing up Sarah's kit: the bib, the bowl, the bottle, the little spoon with Goofy on the hilt.

As Amy passed his table with the tray of coffees the plastic bottle slipped from Jack's hand and bounced on to the floor. He watched, as if in slow motion, as Amy slipped on the bottle and the tray of coffee flew slowly into the air and towards table four. There was an awful inevitability to it as the coffee cups smashed on to the table and drenched the City lads in steaming cappuccino. The men leapt back from the table, their chairs falling behind them, doing a sort of ancient tribal war dance.

'Amy!' screamed the owner, almost about to strike her.

'Don't bother, I'm leaving.' she said as she began pulling her apron off.

Jack stood up to intervene. 'Now wait a minute' he was saying. The owner slammed his bill down on his table.

'You can't fire her for that,' he said.

Amy was already in the kitchen.

'I didn't. She resigned.' The Frenchman shrugged, he didn't seem to care at all what it might mean to her.

'It was my fault.'

'I'm sure it was.'

Amy strode past them, pulling on her coat. Jack reached for Sarah, and his kit bag, and the files. 'Hey, wait. Stop. Wait a minute,' he called, but she was gone. He dashed to the door.

'What about the other bill?' shouted the Frenchman.

Jack turned back. 'You were right. I didn't know them after all.'

He ran into the yard. She had disappeared into the crowd.

Jack left the office mid-afternoon, with a pile of files to read at home. Just as he settled down, the doorbell rang.

Jack was immediately startled, but delighted at the same time. It was William. His hair was combed and he was clean shaven. Even though he was wearing an ill-fitting suit, with a shirt and tie that were never meant to go together, William had most obviously got *himself* together. He looked more like an absent-minded professor now than a tramp.

'William, my God!' exclaimed Jack, smiling broadly.

William gave a little nod. 'I was hoping . . .' he said.

'Yes, of course,' said Jack, holding his hand out to him. 'Won't you come in?'

After William had drunk a cup of tea with him Jack asked him if he might like to take the baby for a spin around the square.

William was obviously delighted, but nodded his head gravely. 'Most certainly, Jack,' he said. 'If that would be a help to you then I should be glad to.'

Jack watched him from the living-room window as William pushed Sarah around the square, all the while chatting to her and singing her nursery rhymes, in the bright afternoon sunshine.

Jack remembered one particular afternoon when they had been very drunk together, hiding behind the hut to avoid the hooligans. William had pulled at some old slats of wood and uncovered a small metal cash box. He took something out. 'Here we are,' he'd said. 'I thought you'd be interested to see this.' He handed Jack a battered black and white photograph.

It was of a quadrangle in an ivy-covered Gothic building. A school. A dozen boys in uniform were standing around a seated figure on a chair. The figure, in black academic gown, was smiling broadly. All the boys wore their boaters at jaunty angles as if nothing in life would ever defeat them.

'My old school,' William had said, slurring and swaying a little. Jack looked at the photograph again.

The seated figure of the housemaster was William.

'Hamforth . . .' said William, smiling, 'not perhaps in the first league. But a happy place. Happy. For a time at least . . .' He grabbed the photograph back, and without looking at it, threw it back into the metal cash box. He gave a short sharp laugh, acknowledging the foolishness of keeping such a picture.

On Friday evening of the next week there was a leaving do for Franklin, one of the oldest partners at WW&P. It would mean a lot to Franklin if Jack could attend, Anna told him.

Franklin was rather wet-eyed as they presented him with a case of wine and a framed picture of St Ives, where he was retiring with his wife. He had served the firm most of his life. He spoke of his nervousness, and his initial opposition, to the move to these new glass and steel offices in the mid-eighties. He spoke of how the company had been a second family to him, and how he wouldn't have wished the course of his life to have gone any other way. He spoke falteringly of the security, and the comradeship, that the legal profession had afforded him, and how Cynthia and himself were looking forward to a restful retirement, mucking about in boats. Maybe, even, inspired by the 'beautiful and thoughtful picture,' taking up water-colours.

Jack looked down, for a moment, to the baby in his arms, and tried to project himself forward thirty years. He could see nothing but a great blank. Certainly not water-colouring in St Ives. He felt keenly aware of what Sarah and he had been robbed of.

Franklin took out his handkerchief and the thirty or so people in the room applauded his speech.

Anna came over with a glass of wine for Jack. He was looking rather lost. She had a mischievous smile on her face.

'You've turned the place into a crêche. You're getting away with murder and you know it,' she said.

'Oh Anna . . .'

She chuckled, rather uncharacteristically. 'Oh, don't get me wrong. I don't mind. It's just interesting, that's all,' she said, surveying the room. 'It would never've happened if you'd been a woman.'

It was true, thought Jack. It was something more than just the novelty of a man with a baby. Such exceptions would never be made for a woman. It was unjust, but she was right.

Howard, a middle-aged man, one of the partners from the northern office, came over.

'Hello, Jack, how are you?'

'Fine, fine. Very well in fact.'

'Is he yours?' the man asked, stroking the baby on the head.

'Yes, she is.'

'And how's Sarah, is she here?' There was a terrible silence. Jack could feel the blood draining from his face. There was suddenly a terrible thudding in his head and stomach and he was plunged back into an overwhelming feeling of despair. Anna took the northern partner by the elbow.

'Howard, can I have a quick word with you,' she said, and she led him away, as if for a conference, to the other side of the room. Jack laid his wine glass down, he felt something like a leper, an untouchable. He glanced at Howard, across the room, who seemed to be visibly shaking with shock.

Jack slipped out of the party. As he was putting Sarah into her car seat he felt a hand on his shoulder. It was Anna.

'Are you all right?' she said.

He most patently wasn't. 'Yeah, I'm fine. You should see the other guy,' he said.

'Seriously . . .'

'Seriously, it's bound to happen. It'll happen again. It's just that one never knows when. Just hits you a bit left of field. I'm fine, honestly.'

'What I said . . .'

'Don't worry. You were right. It's not a problem, I've already made up my mind to get a nanny.'

'OK, if that's what you think is best.' She put her hands on his shoulders and looked at him warmly. Then she kissed him on the lips. Though her mouth was warm, he still felt a coldness throughout his body from the encounter with Howard, and a deeper coldness still from the experience of the last months.

'Good night,' said Anna. 'I'll see you on Monday'.

'Monday . . .' he repeated. Every day was so long to endure right now, it seemed years away.

14

On Saturday morning the doorbell rang. Jack's parents were on the step. His mother was holding a garden fork and a trowel, behind her stood Michael with rhododendrons in pots cradled in his arms.

'We've got these from your father's gardening club, darling and we thought they might just be perfect in your garden.'

'Oh, right, come in,' said Jack. He could barely see his father behind the foliage.

'Once shrubs are established there's no maintenance and they'll transform a little garden like yours. You weren't going out, were you?'

'No, no,' said Jack, 'I was just planning to spend a quiet day at home, alone, with Sarah.'

'Well, that's perfect then, isn't it? We can all do that. Now, why don't you put the kettle on while I sort out my gardening gloves.'

It soon became apparent that the garden gloves were more of a costume than a practical necessity. Margaret's gardening consisted of sitting in a flowery folding chair directing Michael and Jack as she held Sarah on her knee, wrapped in a blanket.

'You want to lop that lilac right back. Don't show it any mercy,' she said.

'But it's about to flower,' Jack protested.

'No matter to that,' said Margaret, 'every bloom you lop off now will come back double next year.' This was, thought Jack, the mating call of the middle classes.

Digging trenches for the shrubs was hard going as the soil was largely made up of the rubble that Nathaniel had pulled from the house. There was evidence of earlier building work too. Michael and Jack struggled to raise an old Victorian sink, followed by what appeared to be the foundations of an Anderson shelter. Solid concrete like a seam of granite. After two hours cursing the ground, and minor disputes about how to go about it flaring up between father and son, they were allowed a break. Margaret handed them mugs of tea.

She looked at her son and smiled. Ah ha, thought Jack, she's building up to something.

'So how is it going at the office?' she asked.

'Fine,' he said.

'And Sarah, you're coping? You must be exhausted.'

'No more than anyone else with a small baby.'

Now she was coming to it. She smiled that thin, ruminative, smile. 'Most people don't have to work at the same time, and if they do, they have help,' she said.

'I'm getting plenty of help at work. Everyone's been extraordinary. They're all chipping in,' he said.

She didn't seem to believe him at all. 'Mmm ... .' she hummed, 'the novelty'll soon wear off.'

'Oh, you're such a cynic,' he said. A baby daughter could hardly be described as a novelty.

She ignored this, and prepared to move to the second heading on her agenda.

'Is it me, or has it turned nippy out here, why don't we go inside?'

The garden was abandoned, looking something like the final stages of the battle of the Somme.

Once inside Margaret began.

'I called my friend Felicity, you know the one I play bridge with in Fulham.'

'Uh huh,' said Jack nervously.

'She runs a nanny agency in Knightsbridge and she's very kindly agreed to send some of her girls over for us to have a look at.'

Jack instinctively reached to take Sarah from her arms.

'What?' he said. 'Wait a minute. One: I don't want a nanny from an agency in Knightsbridge; a) because she'll be a snob and b) because they'll charge me a fortune. Two: I'll fix up my own nanny thank you very much, and three: what's all this about "us"?'

Margaret looked at him unperturbed.

'I can see you're back at work' she said.

They did a little more perfunctory gardening and then Margaret declared that they had to be off. 'Now that we've given you a start.'

Margaret and Michael walked to their car, which they'd taken to parking on the other side of the square in case Jack should see them arrive, and pretend to be out.

Michael was shaking his head.

'You're interfering,' he said at last. She marched on ahead to the car. When Michael caught up he held the keys in his hand, refusing to unlock the car until he'd faced her with it. Margaret looked at the pavement, sighed, and turned to her husband.

'Well if we can't look after the baby then we'll damn well get someone we approve of. Besides that, he's very vulnerable, we can't let him get the wrong sort of help.'

'And what exactly is the "wrong sort"?'

'The sort that chases him all over the house with her knickers wrapped round her ankles. Now open the door.' They drove off in silence. A bit of that sort of thing might not do his son any harm at all, he thought.

By Sunday evening, and after various lengthy phone conversations with his mother, Jack had given in to the idea of interviews being held for a nanny the following Saturday. It was to be run, it appeared, along similar lines as a Commons Select Enquiry, or the McCarthy trials of the fifties.

Jack placed his own advert, however, in *Time Out*. An ad which ran:

'I'm Sarah, I'm three and a half months old and I need a nanny to love me while my daddy is at work . . .'

If nothing else, it would spike up his mother's interviews.

Margaret and Phil arrived together on the Saturday afternoon. It was almost as if they'd had a little conference together beforehand. Michael had been exempted from the interviews on the grounds that he had no experience of such things. Obviously quite glad to be let off the hook, he'd taken himself off to the match at Twickenham.

It had been agreed that the '*Time Out* bunch', as Margaret called them, should be seen first, before they got down to the serious business of Felicity's recommendations. Margaret was dressed as if she was attending a Buckingham Palace garden party. 'We have to give her the right impression,' she said, defending her voluminous floral frock and hat, 'let her know what sort of standards we expect, what sort of people we are.'

It was almost as if they were the ones being

interviewed. It was just the same sort of attitude that had Margaret scrubbing her house spotless whenever the cleaning lady was due.

The first interviewee was twenty minutes late, and they sat staring at the empty chair which Margaret had placed on the far side of the room. She took great delight in looking at her watch and tutting.

'Shall I make us all some more tea?' offered Phil.

'No, dear,' said Margaret, 'we wouldn't want to get ourselves into a position where we may have to offer her one. Should she arrive.'

She did arrive. She was a large girl, about twenty-five, and as Jack opened the door to her so two young children dashed from behind her skirts into the house.

'Sorry I'm a bit late,' she said breathlessly 'had a bugger of a time of it with the kids.' Not the opening line I'd have chosen, thought Jack.

He followed her nervously into the living-room. She plonked herself on to the sofa next to Phil, while her children wandered about, snarling at each other. One of them could have spat for England.

Margaret simply stared at her, regarding her like the women she'd seen on the news living in camps outside American nuclear bases. She wore a brooch with a cannabis leaf on it. Jack found himself perching uneasily on the chair reserved for the interviewee.

'So,' he said, 'have you had much experience in, er, looking after children?'

'Much?' she said enthusiastically. 'I've had custody of these two for the last six months.'

There was a silence as she reached into her bag for a cigarette.

Margaret had no intention of speaking to her at all.

Phil cleared her throat, 'What will you do with, um, your own children?'

'Well, I was hoping to bring them with me,' the woman said. She looked around the room. 'It's a big house, isn't it?' she said. 'Is it flats or all the floors?'

'All the floors,' said Jack. My God, she already had an eye on moving in.

Margaret was staring out of the window, distancing herself entirely from the whole business.

It was difficult. How long do you politely have to prolong a thing like this, thought Jack. She'd dragged herself all across London with these kids. She'd sounded fine on the phone, not that he really knew what he was listening for.

He looked at Sarah, laying in her Moses basket.

'Would you mind not smoking?' he said. 'It's not good for babies.'

The woman stubbed her cigarette out onto a little glass dish that they'd bought on their honeymoon in Venice. Then she stood up briskly. 'Oh, I'm sorry,' she said. 'The ad in *Time Out* didn't say anything about it being non-smoking. It usually says if it is, in *Time Out*. I'm sorry, though, I couldn't take a job where I can't have my fags. I'd go up the wall. You should have said. So I'm sorry, but I'm going to have to turn you down. Sorry about that.'

Margaret looked up. 'I'm sure we'll manage to get over our disappointment eventually' she said.

'Well that's all right then. Hope you get fixed up.'

She swept out of the room, at first forgetting the children.

'Well,' said Jack, 'I think we must have failed to create the right impression, Mother.'

'How many more of these do we have to see?'

'Just two.'

Margaret braced herself as the doorbell rang again.

The other two were equally unsuitable, and Jack was regretting the whole sorry business. One was a rather sullen girl, dressed all in black with a ring through her nose. When Phil asked her if she had a permanent boyfriend she said, 'No, just sort of several, really.'

As she made no effort whatsoever to get the job Jack didn't feel too bad about bringing the interview swiftly to an end.

The last was a nice enough young woman, with neatly cropped hair, but she suddenly dropped it into the conversation that she'd only be able to do three days a week. She was a sculpture student at the Royal College of Art, which would obviously take up some of her time as well. She showed them a little polaroid photograph of one of her works in progress. It was a monstrous rusting thing made from the remains of an industrial boiler.

'One could just imagine her,' said Margaret after she had gone, 'acetylene torch in hand.'

Margaret put the kettle on. At five o'clock, on the dot, there were two pert little rings on the bell. It was Felicity's candidate. This time Margaret went to the door, and led her in.

'Tea?' said Margaret, as her candidate sat on the straight-backed chair.

'Lovely,' she replied, peering at the collection of photographs on the mantelpiece.

'Darjeeling or earl grey?'

'Oh earl grey, absolutely,' she said. She smiled briefly and confidently at Jack and Phil. The living-room had passed. She was a rather efficient-looking woman, in her mid-thirties. She sat rigid in her Guernsey and pearls.

Margaret handed her a cup of tea, and she held the porcelain cup with one hand beneath the saucer and two fingers pinching the delicate handle, as if she was trying to inflict pain upon it. Jack didn't recognise the teacup. He wondered if his mother had brought it with her.

Margaret sat down. 'You come very highly recommended,' she said. 'Lovely references. My friend at your agency, Felicity, was full of praise.'

'Yes,' she said, confidently, and gave a little snort, 'she likes to call me her "no-nonsense" nanny.'

Phil cleared her throat, a little terrified of her. 'Does that mean you're strict with children?'

She threw her head towards Phil. 'No, it means I'm extremely strict with parents.'

She paused for effect and then she let out a long snort. She sounded something like a Dartmoor pony at a Surrey gymkhana.

'No, to be serious,' she said, having thoroughly enjoyed her well-used joke, 'of course baby needs discipline.'

'Her name's Sarah,' said Jack. Since the woman had been in the room, she hadn't even glanced over to the carry-cot.

'What exactly do you mean by "discipline", Miss Cartwright?' asked Phil.

'A routine. Give baby an inch and she'll take a mile,' she said sternly.

'Her name's Sarah, and she's four months old,' said Jack, miserably. Margaret glared at him.

'Never be fooled by a baby's age, Mr Guscott,' replied Miss Cartwright. She was absolutely imperturbable. She didn't imagine for a moment that this young man would have any say in the matter whatsoever.

The interview continued with Miss Cartwright quizzing Jack on his 'routine' and personal habits. Finally Miss Cartwright concluded the whole thing herself by asking them to give Felicity a 'bell' on Monday, because she had 'other parents to see'.

Jack was convinced that his mother had met and interviewed Miss Cartwright before the interview. There were no other candidates. Margaret sat back, satisfied that it was a clear-cut case.

'Well, Phil. Very impressive, I think,' she said.

'She was certainly efficient.'

Jack returned from seeing her out. 'She was awful,' he said, going over to pick Sarah out of her Moses basket.

'What was it you didn't like exactly?'

'Oh, come on, Mother . . .'

'No, explain what you mean.'

'I don't know . . . it just doesn't feel right. I wouldn't be . . .' he flapped his hands around and turned to Phil. 'Look, I don't want to upset you, Phil, but just imagine what Sarah would think. Sarah walks in that door right now and you say Miss Starch Knickers over there is going to look after your baby. You know what she'd say.'

Margaret looked at her. Phil rubbed her cardigan with her hand.

'Yes, I'm afraid I do.'

Jack handed Sarah to Phil. She put her arms round his neck, and they drew each other close. Phil kissed him. It was a sudden moment of intense intimacy, as they shared the terrible grief they both felt. Margaret sat silently chewing the inside of her lip, somehow excluded.

'She doesn't need someone who's impressive, Mum. She needs someone who'll love her.'

'Well then, why don't you let us look after her? I really don't understand why you're being so obstinate.'

There was the sound of the kitchen door closing, and steps in the hallway. Margaret broke off. More steps.

'Is there someone else in the house?'

'Yes,' said Jack, smiling, 'William.'

'Who he?' asked Margaret. She was looking very perplexed.

'A friend,' said Jack. 'He comes in and helps out now and then. Like you, he thinks all this is very unnecessary. Can't see why he doesn't look after her himself.'

There was a polite knock at the door, and then a polished shoe pushed the door open.

'I've made some tea,' he said, holding a silver tray in front of him, with a selection of biscuits in a little bowl. His hair was cut, and smartly slicked back. He wore a white shirt, tie, and a plain green apron. He looked every inch the 'gentleman's gentleman'.

William put the tray down on the coffee table and looked up. 'It needs a couple of minutes in the pot,' he said. He crossed over to Phil and held his hands out to receive the baby. With her mouth slowly dropping she handed Sarah to him without question. He turned the baby over and deftly smelled her nappy.

Sarah gurgled happily.

'Do excuse us,' said William and swept Sarah out of the room for a change.

Phil stared in astonishment at this extraordinary man. The two women looked at each other.

'Where on earth did you get him from?' asked Margaret.

'A skip,' said Jack.

15

It got to the end of the day in the office and Jack picked up the telephone. He wanted to speak to Phil.

'Hi, Phil, it's Jack.'

'Jack, darling, how are you? How can I help?'

'Just fancied calling you,' he said. 'Look, are you doing anything?'

'No, just sitting here reading through some bumph for a meeting.' Phil was still active in her local CND.

'Do you fancy hitting the town with your grand-daughter and me tonight?'

'What have you got in mind?'

'Oh nothing heavy. It's just the house gets lonely sometimes, and she's growing so fast, we need new ballgowns almost every day. Her rompers have gone at the elbows.'

Phil laughed. 'So?'

'So how's about late night shopping?'

'My God,' said Phil, 'you do live dangerously.'

He arranged to pick her up, and they'd take a bowl down Kensington High Street. He felt for Phil. Pamela had solved her problem about what to do before she went up to university in the autumn. She'd gone back-packing to Turkey. So now Phil was on her own. She'd get a kick out of choosing rompers for her granddaughter and, as long as his mother didn't find out, he'd enjoy her company too.

Sarah had loved shopping. It was her natural element, whether in Bentalls or a Tunisian bazaar, she shopped as if it were a sport. She knew the value of everything. He felt especially lost in department stores without her.

Phil, of course, was not a natural shopper. She tended to turn a thing over to examine its country of origin so that she could make a political decision before splashing out on it. Nevertheless, the babygrow section of the store was a uniting factor for them both. What did it matter if the baby came out of the store looking like a Rainbow Warrior? Jack could almost hear Sarah's voice over his shoulder, saying 'man-made fibre urrgh!', or 'I want it and I have to have it'. Sarah had been right, there was a great release in spending a fortune, 'abusing plastic' as she called it every time she slapped down the Mastercard. 'Plastic in exchange for silk,' was another of her maxims.

She wasn't spoilt, or extravagant, she just wanted to be alive, now, and sometimes that necessarily took the form of purchasing shiny, but absolutely useless, objects of desire.

There was a very particular atmosphere to the department store tonight. It was late night shopping, the pressure was off. The staff chatted with each other as if they were at some sort of cocktail party, clocking up overtime. The clientele was different. The tourists were in the theatres, the office folk were in the hands of Network South East, only the real shopaholics were here. The *crème de la* cashcard.

The whole thing gave Jack a warm feeling. It was good to go out with Phil. He was making it clear to her, he knew, that she didn't have to sneak round to his house on some spurious pretext just to see her granddaughter. He was conscious also that he was desperately filling up empty time, they both were.

They toured the store.

'What about toys?' asked Phil. 'Surely she needs new toys?'

'Babies don't need toys' said Jack.

'But I do,' said Phil. They laughed and went in the lift to the extensive toy department where they admired the revolution that had occurred in the design of water pistols. They now came with three-litre back-packs.

'Surely the little children will fall over backwards with the weight of it,' said Phil.

'These,' said Jack, authoritatively, 'are designed for the dads.' He would really have quite liked one.

The little fluffy ducks, the Mrs Tiggy Winkles, and the musical potties that played when you peed in them, sent them off into paroxysms of joy. Into the basket.

Another shopper joined them before a pyramid of polyester Flintstone characters that yelled 'Yabba Dabba Doo' if you poked them. The man was about thirty-five, and, like the majority of other men in the store, was obviously one of those who'd forgotten to get a birthday present for one of their kids before going home. He smiled at them, looking for reassurance in his purchase.

He looked at Sarah, strapped to Jack's chest.

'Handsome little chap,' he said.

'Thank you,' said Jack, through gritted teeth. The man picked up a four-foot Fred and went to the cash desk.

'Why does everyone think she's a boy?' said Jack. 'She doesn't look like a boy, does she? I mean, she's not butch or anything. Who did he think she was, Bam?'

Phil laughed, he looked so suddenly serious.

'Of course not. You shouldn't let it upset you. It

happens to everyone. They probably thought you were a girl at her age. It'll be different when she's got hair.'

'What do you mean?' said Jack, throwing Dino back into the pyramid.

'When she's got some hair she'll look more like a girl.' Phil chuckled.

Jack was filling with fury. 'She has got hair.'

'I know'

'She's not bald. She's got hair. It's growing. Look at it.'

'I know.'

'She's not bald.'

'I know'

'So what are you saying?'

'Don't be so sensitive.'

'I need some new shirts,' said Jack, turning away. 'Sarah tends to throw up on them after breakfast.'

'Have you tried washing them?' said Phil. Jack laughed. 'You really must get yourself sorted out with a nanny.'

'I know, I know,' he said wearily, as they walked to the lift. As usual the men's department was in the basement. Five floors down. They maintained silence for two floors, then Phil poked him in the ribs and giggled.

'I do love you,' she said, 'because you're a fool. A passionate fool.'

He looked at her for a moment coldly, and then laughed. They grasped each other, laughing, Sarah shrieking between them with delight. Mid-twirl, the lift doors opened on to an elderly couple waiting in the basement. Catching sight of their faces, Jack and Phil finished their twirl and stepped out into the shirt department.

The elderly lady, obviously impressed, made to touch

Phil's arm. 'What a lovely baby you've got,' she said, 'how old is he?' Phil looked at her. 'She's a girl!' she said. 'She's wearing a dress for God's sake. What more do you want, a sign around her neck?'

The elderly couple nipped into the lift and frantically stabbed at the buttons. Phil and Jack marched towards the crisp designer shirts. As Jack, with a wicked smirk on his face, turned towards Phil, she whisked her head away.

'Oh well,' she said, 'she had it bloody coming to her.'

The shirt department was so boring compared to toys. Jack tried to explain the problem to Phil. When the collar is right, the cuffs are wrong. When the linen is right, they screw the whole thing up with some sort of daft embroidery above the breast pocket. Choice is easy for women, they can agonise over it, he said. But when the choice is a half centimetre here or there, it's an imponderable conundrum.

'William was a bit of a shock on Saturday, wasn't he?' said Jack.

'Yes,' said Phil, 'I must admit we were a bit taken aback.'

'I hoped you might be. You see, the trouble with you women is that you think babies are your sole preserve. No one really believes that I can change a nappy as expertly as I do. Not to mention my considerable culinary achievements with the blender.'

Phil held his arm. 'You are a wonderful son,' she said, 'never forget that, a wonderful son and a wonderful father to my granddaughter even if you do get pissed and hire tramps as houseboys.'

'William isn't a houseboy,' said Jack, in mock defensiveness.

'No I know,' said Phil, 'I've seen him in the square

many a time, rummaging in your skip. Thank God Margaret hasn't.'

'Only because she'd have had her nose in the air.'

'Oh, she's not so insensitive, you know. She'd give up everything for you, you know that.'

'Unless, of course, it was her bridge night.' But Jack did know it really, they'd just got themselves stuck into the position of never really being able to express what they felt for each other.

Phil took hold of a shirt Jack was clutching, took a look at its braided front and threw it back. She laughed.

Sarah had begun to wriggle on Jack's chest. It was time for a sudden, and unannounced bawl in a public place. Jack felt her nappy.

'Oh shit,' he said. 'She needs changing.'

'Let me take her to the changing room,' said Phil.

Jack stepped back about two feet. 'I suddenly think this conversation hasn't happened,' he said.

'My God, you're a hard date for a night on the town.'

'I know. No, don't worry, I'll find somewhere, I'll get her changed.'

'No sole preserve,' said Phil, pointedly.

Jack clicked his heels. He glanced towards the lift and the list of departments embossed in gold.

'I'll meet you in electrical appliances in five minutes,' he said, whipping a Pamper from his kit bag. Phil smiled. He gave a flourish of the nappy as he stepped into the lift.

Jack got to the eighth floor and stepped boldly out. It was all poor reproduction Adam fireplaces and the accounts department. Sarah was now in some distress. He saw the sign to the Ladies and Mothers' Room and heaved a sigh of relief.

He made to push the door open. A large, heavy hand fell on his shoulder.

'Excuse me, that's the ladies. The men's room is on the third floor,' said an elderly, military type voice. Jack turned around. It was a security man in dark serge.

'I don't want to use the toilet. I want to change her nappy,' Jack said. The guard looked at the baby incredulously, as if it was something Jack had just purchased in the store and wanted to try out.

'Well you can't go in there,' he said.

'Why not?'

The man bristled. 'Because it's the ladies toilet, that's why not.'

'It is also the changing room,' said Jack, trying to sound eminently reasonable.

'In point of fact it's the mothers' room.'

'What exactly is the difference?'

'It's for mothers. You're not a mother.' Jack nodded calmly.

'This is true. So where is the fathers' room?'

'There isn't one,' said the guard, as if it were a point of pride.

'Well, there you go,' said Jack, and turned back with his hand on the changing room door, 'excuse me.'

The guard grabbed him firmly by the arm.

'If I drop this baby I will sue you, and this store, for every penny you've got. Now let go.' The man's eyes, the guard could see, were deadly serious. He let go.

'You cannot go in there,' he said. Jack spun around.

'Listen. It is not my fault that you only provide facilities for women to change their children and not men. I need to change my daughter's nappy and I'm going to use the room provided. If you don't like it, build another room.'

The man was quiet for a moment.

'I'll have to call the manager,' he said.

'Good, because if you don't, then I will.'

The guard marched off, square-bashing through home furnishings.

'Another blow struck for paternal rights,' said Jack to Sarah as he pushed open the door 'God, I hope there's no one in there.'

He laid Sarah on the changing top. When a lavatory flushed in one of the cubicles he ducked his head low over Sarah, hoping to pass for a young mother in a heavy overcoat. 'Oh, no, do hurry up, hurry up,' he muttered, as if Sarah could help at all in the process.

The woman washed her hands at the far end of the room, picked up her shopping and left. Jack put down his bottle of talc. The door opened and another woman came in. He could sense her standing just a few feet from him, adjusting her hair in the mirror.

'That's the weirdest-looking boy I've ever seen,' said a voice. Jack looked up into the mirror. It was Amy, the waitress from the brasserie.

'Amy?'

She smirked. 'Do you always use the ladies' restroom?'

'Yes,' he said, slightly flustered, 'I mean no. I tried to catch up with you the other day.'

'Oh, don't worry,' she said.

'Well I did. I felt responsible.'

'Don't,' she said brightly, 'it wasn't so much of a job as a punishment from hell. I must've done something really dreadful in a previous life.'

The moment Jack was finished with the nappy Amy picked Sarah up. Sarah's eyes filled with delight as they rubbed noses.

'Are you working, what are you doing now?' asked Jack.

'What's her name?' she said, absorbed in the child.

'Sarah.'

'Nothing. I'm doing nothing at all. Hello, Sarah,' she said, holding her to her face.

16

Jack called the office. 'I'm on my way in now, I'm on my way,' he said frantically to Jackie. 'Just tell Anna that I'm going to have to bring Sarah in today.'

He gripped the receiver with his chin while trying to feed the baby and at the same time fasten cuff links on his new shirt. He was in something of a panic, it was nearly ten o'clock already.

'Well what's happened to this nanny?' asked Jackie.

'I don't know where the fuck she is. She's not turned up. I'll see you in a bit.'

He put the phone down and it rang again immediately.

'Hello?' It was Margaret.

'It's me. Has she arrived yet?'

'No she hasn't.'

'I thought this might happen. Shall I come over?'

'No, I've got to get to work, I can't wait. I'll have to take her with me. Maybe tomorrow.'

'I'll have to check my diary.'

'You do that.'

He put the phone down, and sighed heavily.

The doorbell rang. Don't loose your temper, Jack, whatever her excuse is, don't blow it, he said to himself, walking to the door.

'Amy, you're late,' he said 'which means I'm late!' he shouted.

She stood there smiling, two suitcases beside her on the step.

'I know, I know,' she said. 'I'm sorry. It took me longer than I thought to get my stuff together.'

'Right,' said Jack, his mind still on getting into work. Half-way down the hallway he turned back. 'Stuff? What stuff?' Amy had disappeared. He looked into the square where a taxi driver was unloading more 'stuff' from the cab. Carpet bags, a paper carrier with a vase sticking out of the top of it. Clothes on wire hangers.

'Whoa . . . whoa! Wait a minute!' he shouted. 'What are you doing?' Downstairs he could hear Sarah beginning to cry. 'Shit' he said and dashed down to get her.

When he returned Amy was standing in the hallway surrounded by all her worldly goods. 'Amy, what's going on?'

'I know it seems a lot but once it's in my room you'll never know it's here.'

Jack stared at the bags, swallowed, and looked at her.

'Your room?' he said. 'This is a daily job. The ad clearly stated "daily".'

'I didn't see any ad. If I remember right, you offered me the job in a ladies toilet.'

'But you can't stay here. You just work here.'

'I see,' said Amy.

They both surveyed her luggage again.

'I thought . . .'

The telephone rang again.

'That'll be the office,' he said in exasperation, 'I've got to go. We'll sort this out later.' He handed her a nappy, that he'd grabbed when he picked Sarah up. 'She needs a change.'

'A change?' said Amy, a look of puzzled amusement on her face.

'Yes, her nappy. You have changed a nappy before?'

She looked at him blankly, as if he was suddenly speaking Chinese.

'You know, her thing, her . . .' he searched for the correct Americanism, 'her diaper.'

'Oh right, her diaper, sure.'

Jack handed the baby to her and dashed down the steps towards the tube. It'd be quicker than the traffic.

Amy carried Sarah in her arms. She looked into the living-room. It was a rather cold room and looked unused. She went down the stairs to the basement. Ah, this was better, obviously the room in the house where all the actual 'living' was done. It was all very open-plan and cosy. She was rather daunted, however, by the great mass of 'baby things' laying around. They were obviously a lot more complex than she'd imagined when she agreed to the job in the department store.

She laid Sarah on the draining board, gripping the diaper in her teeth. She tugged at the existing nappy. Finally it came free and she pulled it off. What she found was something of a shock to her.

'Oh God . . .' she said, holding her nose and looking away. It was appalling, it was disgusting. She looked at Sarah's sweet little face. How the hell could such a perfect-looking thing . . . ?

Jack charged into the office, throwing off his coat. The telephone on his desk was already festooned with little yellow Post-it notes, detailing the calls he'd missed. Jackie caught his coat and hung it up, a swathe of papers for him in her arms. He sat down at his desk and surveyed it.

'She turned up then,' said Jackie. 'Coffee?'

'I think perhaps I should call,' he said, grabbing the receiver.

'You've only just arrived.'

'Even so, she doesn't know where anything is.' He began dialling. 'I haven't had time to show her the ropes. I'll just make sure she's settled in.'

He looked up at Jackie. 'It's engaged!'

'Sounds like she's settled in to me,' said Jackie.

Amy was, indeed, on the telephone. She had called Los Angeles. Sarah was still laying unchanged on the draining board.

'I know it's four-thirty in the morning, Mom . . .' she was saying '. . . but it's an emergency . . . no, no, I'm fine, it's just that I don't know how to change a diaper . . .' She held the phone from her ear for a moment. Then she spoke again. 'Mom, calm down, calm down . . . I haven't had a baby. I've got a job. I'm a nanny . . . what's so funny about that?' Her mother was laughing hysterically at the other end.

Jack dialled again and gave up. He took his portable phone out of his desk drawer and took it out to Jackie.

'Have this sent round to my house on a bike will you?'

Jackie shook her head. 'She's bound to get off the phone soon.'

'What if she goes out? I won't be able to get hold of her. Anything could happen. Now just send it round. Please?'

Jack went back to sit at his desk. Maybe he should have hired Miss Starch Knickers after all. No, no, he was

138

overreacting. It would all be fine. He began returning the calls on the Post-its.

Amy was somewhat surprised by the arrival of the mobile phone but after she'd thought about it she could see that it wasn't such a bad idea. So she took it as a cue to call her former flatmate, Susan, and arrange to meet her for lunch. Surely the little baby would soon get bored sitting around the house all day. Babies need a constant round of new sights and sounds to stimulate them, and a pizzeria in Islington High Street would be just the thing, she thought. Yes, maybe she'd make a nanny after all.

Susan was one of her oldest friends and they'd travelled to Europe together. Like a lot of close friends, they were opposites in many respects. Where Amy was blonde, and slim, Susan was brunette and rather ebullient. She took life very much as it came. Her parents were wealthy and had bank-rolled her travels, paying as well for a rather grand apartment in a warehouse in the City. She'd turned it into something reminiscent of a New York loft. Hardly any furniture, but lots of drapes.

They had a leisurely lunch. Susan was amazed by Amy's career change from waitress to nanny.

'How do you know what to do with her?' she asked.

'Experience,' said Amy, sitting with the baby on her lap holding the bottle to her mouth.

'Come on, Amy, experience – you?'

'OK, so I called my mom.'

Susan laughed. The whole project was sounding more unlikely by the minute. 'What's the house like?'

'Nice, it's very nice. I think that's what you call houses in England, and it's very English. Trendy, though. His wife had good taste.'

'His wife?'

'Yeah. She died. She died when Sarah was born.'

'Shit, that's tragic,' said Susan. 'What's your room like?'

Amy hesitated for a moment. 'It's fine.'

'Isn't it going to be a bit weird living with this guy on your own?'

'We have a terrific chaperon. Anyway, I don't hear you offering my room back. How is Alain?'

Susan played with the remnants of the garlic bread.

'He's great,' she said at last, 'were you ever this happy with him?'

'For about half an hour.' Susan stared into her face. She could always tell when Amy was hurting about something, because she always covered it over with a smart remark.

'Why aren't you angry with me?' she asked.

'Who says I'm not?' They smiled and Susan squeezed her hand.

Margaret had called Jack in the office. She'd been calling his home all morning.

'She's probably taken the baby out for a walk. Don't be so neurotic,' said Jack.

Jackie stood by his office door shaking her head in amusement.

'So what shall we do?' asked Margaret.

' "We"?'

'A complete stranger is roaming the streets of London with your child and you're going to do nothing. Well, on your head be it.' Margaret rang off. Jack dialled the number of his mobile.

Susan turned to Amy, a surprised look on her face.

'I hate to tell you this, but your buggy is ringing,' she said.

'Oh God, can you pass it over?' Susan handed her the mobile phone, which had been tucked under Sarah's pillow. 'Hello,' she said wearily.

'You're not at home,' said Jack, abruptly. He could hear music, and voices in the background.

'Correct.'

He reminded himself to tread carefully with her. He didn't want to give the impression that he was at all neurotic about his baby.

'Fine, that's OK. That's good' he said.

Amy led him flounder at the other end for a moment. He was probably going to need more training than the baby.

'Was there any particular purpose to this call?'

'Um yes . . .' Jack thought quickly. 'I want you to bring her into work.'

'What, now?'

'Yes,' said Jack, trying to sound as sure as he could of his own mind.

Amy gave it another beat. 'But I thought the whole point of me was that you didn't have to take her to work.'

Jack nodded to himself. 'Yes . . . You're right, of course you're right . . . Put her on, will you?'

'What?'

'The baby. I want to speak to her. Put her next to the phone.'

'OK . . .'

Amy took the bottle from Sarah's mouth. Susan was watching the whole performance, quite mesmerised. This guy was weird. Amy held the phone by the baby's ear.

Susan was beginning to giggle. A waiter passed and stared. Amy put the phone back to her ear.

'All right?' she said.

'Why's she breathing so heavily?' Jack asked.

'She's excited. She's never been on the phone before.'

'Where exactly are you?'

'In a café with my friend Susan.'

The smile dropped from Susan's face, as if to say 'don't involve me in this'.

Jack thought for a moment.

'Does she smoke?' he asked.

'No she doesn't smoke.'

'So you're in the non-smoking section?'

'I don't know.' There was no one in the restaurant smoking at all, so it was difficult to tell.

Jack grunted.

'I don't want her surrounded by smoke.'

'That's very sweet of you,' said Amy, looking at Susan, 'but she's twenty-six and quite capable of looking after herself.'

'I'm talking about . . .'

'I know who you're talking about. Listen, she's . . .' Then Amy pressed the button on the receiver and laid the phone face down on the table.

'You cut him off!' said Susan.

'That's the fifth call this morning,' she said.

'Well, he's obviously concerned . . .'

'Don't worry, he'll think we went under a bridge.'

'In a restaurant?' said Susan.

Jackie had rather enjoyed watching Jack tie himself up in knots. He now looked so shocked.

'She cut me off. She cut me off!' he said. Jackie felt that

she might, after all, be able to establish a working relationship with this girl.

Jack threw himself into his work for the rest of the afternoon.

When Margaret discovered that the nanny had finally hauled herself back to Jack's house she thought it would be a good idea to pop round. She could help with teatime. Show her the way the kitchen worked, that sort of thing.

The door was opened by William, smart in his green apron.

'Oh, good afternoon,' said Margaret, 'I didn't expect . . . I suppose you thought you'd lend a hand on her first day.'

'Yes, lend a hand . . .' said William, mysteriously. He led her down to the kitchen. Something seemed to have put his nose out of joint.

Margaret's first impression was that she might be a little too glamorous for the task in hand. Glamorous was one of those expressions Margaret reserved for the type of girl she'd already described to Michael, when he'd refused to open the car door. This girl was far too pretty, she thought, to ever be taken seriously as a nanny. She wouldn't last the week.

She introduced herself formally. The girl looked nervous. She was in the middle of changing Sarah's nappy, and seemed quite flustered by the business. Margaret watched her from the other side of the kitchen. She tried not to exude the air of someone adjudicating a home economics class too much, but it was an uphill struggle.

Phil arrived.

The nappy was taking quite a time to change.

'I think you'll find that's the wrong way round' said William at last.

Amy steadied herself. Took a deep breath in.

'Oh yes, so it is. Thank you, Bill.'

William winced.

She turned to him, smiling as politely as she could.

'Can you pass me those trousers?' she said. Margaret moved in.

'I think she'd like to wear a dress today,' she said in her sweetest voice.

Amy put her into a dress.

'There we are,' she said, as brightly as she could when it was done. 'I think it's time madam had a little sleep. She's tired.'

'She's not tired, dear, she's bored. She needs entertaining,' said Phil.

'Fine. Well, would you mind entertaining her while I do her washing?' she said, trying to keep her temper and her voice as reasonably businesslike as possible.

'It's done,' said William's voice from behind.

'Oh, right. Thanks. Well, I'll get on with her dinner then.' As she said this she heard the sound of the blender being switched on. She turned to smile at William. She smiled as best she could.

17

It was Friday afternoon. Jack had not looked forward to the weekend for so long, but today he spent the last hour of work looking continually at his watch. He alternated it with gazing out of the window. Across the street was a register office and a young couple, just married, were having their photographs taken in the late afternoon sunshine. He smiled at them. Wished them luck. They looked so full of hope.

He was excited about spending the weekend alone with Sarah. Amy would be out flat-hunting. It would just be the two of them.

He raced home.

He burst in the front door, threw his keys down, and trotted down the stairs.

'Hi, I'm home . . . hello?' he called.

He was already taking his jacket and tie off, signalling to himself the start of the weekend. The house was empty. Where were they? He put the kettle on and went to the cupboard for a mug. There wasn't one. Every mug he possessed, along with much of the rest of the crockery, was lying unwashed in the sink. The dishwasher was full as well, and hadn't been switched on. He tripped on one of Sarah's toys that was laying on the kitchen floor. He reached for the jar of coffee. It was empty. He looked around the room. It was a mess. The bin was overflowing. The nappy sack was full.

He flopped on to the sofa, still holding his empty mug as the kettle boiled.

He watched the evening news, miserably. It had been a very long week since Amy's arrival. He'd found it harder than he thought it would be to have a woman in the house. There were items of her clothing lying in a laundry basket, and he despised them for not being his wife's.

Jack tried to snap himself out of it. It was he, after all, who'd begged her to do this job. It wasn't her fault she wasn't Sarah. He was being unreasonable.

He went to take a sip from his mug. Damn her.

Finally the front door opened, and his heart leapt at the thought of seeing his daughter. He could hear the sound of rustling carrier bags, and a struggle with the front door. Amy came bounding down the stairs.

'Hi, sorry I'm late. Been shopping.'

'Oh good. We're out of quite a few things.'

'What?' said Amy. 'Oh no, no – baby shopping. I got her some stuff for the summer. Really cute. We had fun.'

'Ah, ha,' said Jack, 'and where is she?' Amy stared at him blankly.

'Where's Sarah!' he yelled.

Amy looked momentarily blank. My God, had she left her in the shop?

Amy said nothing but ran back up the stairs into the street.

'I was about to take her home,' said the taxi driver, coming up the steps with her. She took the baby, unable to speak, and ran back down to Jack.

'God, I'm sorry, Jack. I'm really, really, sorry. God, how terrible. It was all the bags. It won't happen again. I promise it won't happen again.'

'Don't worry about it,' said Jack sarcastically. It was a pleasure to see her looking quite so mortified.

'It was just all the bags. So much stuff, and rushing back. I don't know how I did that,' said Amy.

He remembered a story Phil had told him. When Sarah had been a baby she'd left her, pram and all, in Woolworths. A policeman had brought her home. He reminded himself that if a mother could do this, and Sarah's own mother at that, it wasn't so terrible a crime for a nanny to commit. Worrying though it was.

But Amy's mortification didn't last long. She began pulling things out of her carrier bags. There was a little denim outfit, like the sort of thing a welder or a mechanic might wear, but scaled down. It was almost identical to the clothes Amy was wearing, in fact.

'Isn't it just adorable?' said Amy, obviously impressed by her purchase. 'Look I got a hat as well. It matches, see?' She plonked a little, floppy, denim hat on Sarah's head. 'Doesn't she just look edible in it?' It was obvious that she'd had a wild afternoon spending Jack's money. But it was rather as if Amy had been dressing a doll.

Jack nodded quietly.

Amy sighed at how wonderful Sarah looked.

'Listen,' she said, turning swiftly to Jack, 'there wasn't enough in the pot so you owe me.'

'No problem,' said Jack, keeping his temper even and reaching for the wallet in his jacket pocket, over the back of the chair. 'How much?'

'Two sixty,' she said pertly.

'Oh, right,' he said, replacing his wallet and reaching into his trouser pocket for some change. He counted out the coins.

'Um . . .' a worried expression suddenly crossed her face, 'Um . . . hundred. Two hundred and sixty.'

'What?! Two hundred and sixty pounds?'

'I know, I know,' replied Amy immediately, 'I was surprised. I could hardly believe it myself. A few little outfits and bits and pieces. I asked them to check and there it was, sure enough, two hundred and sixty. It'd be cheaper in the States.'

'It'd be cheaper to go to the States,' snapped Jack.

Amy nodded in agreement. She held Sarah out to him. 'Can you take her? I've got to go. I'm late.' He seemed to be unable to speak. 'I'm going out' she said. 'You did say you wanted to bath her tonight. It being the weekend and everything.'

'Yes, yes, that's right.'

'Great, I'll just grab a sandwich.' She went over to the fridge, grabbed some cheese, and a tomato from the salad box. Then she flapped around looking for some bread. Failing, she gnawed on the cheese, and ate the tomato.

'So how have you found your first week?' asked Jack.

'Terrific,' she said, 'everybody's been . . . very helpful.' She sounded like he did when he was lying through his teeth to a client, or his mother. He picked up a pile of estate agent's bumph from the worktop.

'I see you've been looking for a flat.'

She finished off her tomato, pips running down her chin.

'No, not me,' she said. 'Your mother left them for me this afternoon. See you later.' She dashed upstairs to change.

Jack sat down with Sarah on the sofa. Well, this was it, their weekend together. He listened to Amy crashing about upstairs. The first week hadn't really gone as well as he'd hoped. Perhaps it wasn't just enough to be 'natural' with the child. While little Sarah seemed eminently comfortable in Amy's company, he didn't know that he was. She'd invaded, that's what she'd done. Not just his house, but his life as well. Not just life as it was now, either. She was, in effect, trampling over Sarah's memory, over the space that his wife still had in his life. Trampling with her T-shirts, and her bras in the laundry basket.

He wondered where she was going, what life there was of hers beyond that front door. He wished she would go to it quickly.

'Bye,' came a voice, and the front door slammed. She was probably relieved to be away, he thought. He was such a mixture of emotions again. He wished he could settle on something in the middle, but once again, it was all extremes. Painful extremes.

Jack enjoyed putting Sarah to bed, in her cosy little nursery, but when she'd gone to sleep he felt a little empty in the house alone. He sat by her crib, staring at her, waiting for her to wake up tomorrow. The only thing he could think to do now was go to bed himself, even though it was only ten-thirty.

At one in the morning he woke up suddenly. There was the sound of doors slamming as Amy crashed about the house. Then the house went quiet until he heard a stirring from the nursery. He could hear Sarah whimpering. He grabbed the duvet around him and staggered off to see her.

Small though she was, she'd managed to get the bedclothes into a knot around her. He untangled his child and stroked her forehead until she calmed. For a while her little hand was clasped in his. She went back to sleep.

As he walked to his bedroom he passed Amy's door. It was ajar and he glanced in. She was lying face down, the duvet pulled away to her waist. Her naked back, in the moonlight, looked smooth and perfect. She slept perfectly still. Her skin was as smooth as Sarah's, baby Sarah's.

Jack threw himself on to his bed.

He was up again at six a.m. Sarah was crying.

'Oh darling,' he pleaded, 'you don't want to be up already do you? Please, you want to go back to sleep, don't you?' She stopped crying and looked up at him, bright eyed and bushy-tailed.

Jack dismissed all thoughts of going back to sleep. 'OK then, let's have a bath.' She was too adorable.

The two of them made a great deal of noise, for a lawyer and a baby, a few gallons of water and a couple of ducks.

Sarah was a wonderful little thing, and a great way to greet the day. He dried her in his great big bath towel, almost losing her in it, and took her into his bedroom, to lie in towels and cuddle.

Jack stared out of the window into the square. It was almost May, and the trees of the park were budded still with pink. The wind had driven the fallen blossom into heaps like snow. The grass was checkered with clumps of daffodils. Sarah seemed to give a great softness to everything.

They went downstairs at about eleven. Amy was laying on the sofa reading a magazine.

'Hi,' said Jack. He felt warm and in quite good spirits, Sarah had charmed him so much.

'Hi,' said Amy.

'Sleep well?'

'Like a baby,' she said.

He turned to Sarah. 'Hear that?' he chuckled.

'Do you want me to have her?' There was a slightly pained, but business-like look on Amy's face.

'No, it's the weekend. Relax. You don't have to do a thing,' he said cheerily. Jack went over to the washing machine and began sorting out the chaos that surrounded it. He glanced over to Amy, lying full stretch on the sofa. His expression began to change. Why was she just lolling there? Surely she had loads of things she wanted to do with her first weekend off?

She had all the Saturday newspapers around her and was picking at a pile of toast. She'd obviously made it to the shop this morning, thought Jack. He listened to the way she crunched at the toast. There's no way to eat toast without crunching, he admitted, but nevertheless, it was still irritating. Stupidly annoying this morning.

'So what have you got planned for the weekend?' he said as casually as he could.

'Nothing. I just thought I'd hang out.' She turned back to her newspaper and took another crunch of toast.

'Amy,' he said, 'I don't want to upset you or anything, but this isn't going to work.'

'What?' She was bemused, his voice had gone serious all of a sudden.

'This,' he said, looking around the room in general.

'This what?'

'Your being here. Now. Just sitting there.'

She crunched again and looked perplexed. She didn't understand what he wanted from her at all. She stared at him, slightly lost.

'But you just told me not to do anything,' she said.

151

'I know, yes. I don't want you to do anything, but I'd rather you didn't do it somewhere else.'

Her face dropped. 'Oh . . . right,' she said flatly and folded the newspaper she was reading and stood up.

'You do understand,' said Jack. 'I just need some space. Some time on my own. Just me and Sarah.' He tried to smile. He felt terrible, but it had to be said.

'Sure,' said Amy, walking to the stairs, knowing that she'd better take herself out. He looked suddenly very uncomfortable about it, but it was obvious that he meant it.

'Don't look so upset,' she said, trying to retrieve the situation, 'no one's died.'

Jack's face went rigid.

Amy felt as if she'd just given him an electric shock. It was, she knew, one of the most stupid things she'd ever said in her life. They stared at each other for a few moments. There was a heaviness in the air between them.

'I think I'd better go,' said Amy, guiltily. Jack couldn't speak.

She let herself out, closing the door uncharacteristically quietly behind her.

She sat on the tube train, shaking her head. This job was nowhere as easy as she'd imagined when she took it on.

She looked around her. She didn't like the London Underground, it seemed to make everyone look tired and impatient. Not only that but the designers had made it so that you had to stare at each other like reflections of one's own unease.

A class of French schoolchildren on an educational break burst on for two stops and ran up and down the aisles, shouting in high-pitched voices. Then the carriage returned to its droning silence, the only human sound was the tinging and the clashing of the percussion track coming from the Walkman of the boy next to her. It irritated her like flies buzzing around her head.

Every station looked just like the last, dirty and inhospitable, the same ads on the billboards, variations on the same dated designs on the ceramic tiles. For the country that gave birth to the train they sure as hell have tried to bury it, she thought.

Finally she got off and walked to Susan's warehouse. She buzzed the entryphone.

'Hello, it's me. Can I come up?'

There was no answer just the sound of shrieking.

'Oh hi . . .' said Susan's voice, breathlessly. 'Look it's kinda . . . not convenient . . .' Susan screamed and giggled again. 'Stop it, stop it . . .' she was saying.

A young guy passed her as she stood staring into the battered metal grille of the entryphone. He sniggered at her as the obvious sounds of Saturday afternoon sex were broadcast into the street.

'Alain . . . stop it . . .' screeched Susan.

Amy walked forlornly away, kicking at the litter blowing on the pavement. At this rate she'd be whiling away her afternoon with American tourists at the London Planetarium, or something equally bizarre. Maybe she could catch up with those French schoolkids.

Jack was looking out into the square and smiling, watching William raking up leaves and blossom, inspecting each shrub as if he'd planted them himself. Since William's 'reformation', he'd become quite a busy man. With Jack's intervention the local council had found him accommodation, and the residents' committee had appointed him to part-time work helping out with the 'husbandry' of the square, as William called it. He still helped out at Jack's too, fitting them into his busy schedule, on alternate afternoons. It was a pleasure for Jack to see that something good had come of a hard time.

It was difficult to tell what had caused such a radical transformation in William. Perhaps it had been a shock watching Jack descend so swiftly to his own drunken, degenerate state. As if he'd dragged one of his old pupils down with him, and it had shaken him.

Jack watched him attacking the shrubbery with secateurs. The causes of his drinking were still there, of course. He'd taken to gardening, and Sarah's laundry, with that same obsessive streak that had probably driven him to drink in the first place. It was better to be addicted to housework, naturally, but it was just as obsessive for William.

Then the doorbell rang, breaking Jack's solitary bliss. It was the first time, really, that he'd been able to settle into his new house, as himself, with his child in this new life. But the chance to do it was brief.

He opened the front door.

'Mum?!' he said, surprised.

She stared at him for a moment.

'Oh it's so gratifying when he recognises me,' she said.

Michael was hovering on the step behind her. 'What is it?' he said.

'Please let us in, darling. The neighbours'll think we're Jehovah's Witnesses.'

He moved aside as she marched formally into the hallway.

'Well obviously, as it's the weekend we thought you'd need a hand,' she said.

Amy wandered along the Embankment, watching the Thames as it flowed, grey and heavy. She passed Cleopatra's Needle, it too looked grey and heavy, and in an alien land. She'd never done the 'touristy' bit since she'd been in London, and really didn't want to be driven to it now. She sat on a bench for a while.

The wrought iron bench was Victorian, and very grand for a bench, with ornate scrolls, and lion's feet. But underneath it lay an empty, overturned, bottle of VP sherry, left by a tramp. It gave her the overwhelming feeling of being suddenly stranded, down and out, in this city. She lived in one room of a house in which she wasn't wanted. Even her clothes couldn't find space in the wardrobe, where Sarah's still hung in polythene, suffocating, where they'd been abandoned since the day of the move. She hadn't liked to discuss it with Jack.

She watched a young couple coming towards her, laughing, arm in arm.

'Excuse me,' said the girl, offering her a camera, 'would you take a photograph of us?'

'Sure,' said Amy. The young couple posed, leaning against the railing, with the Thames behind. She despised them. Couples were hateful when they wanted complete strangers to record their happiness. How did they know that she wasn't sitting here, waiting for them to pass so that she could throw herself in the river?

Amy was a little depressed today.

Not an hour after Margaret arrived Jack was called to the door again.

'There was a meeting in the square about the closure of the library,' said Phil.

'Yes?' said Jack, wondering what possible relevance this had to anything.

'Well, as I went I thought I might as well drop in.'

'This square?'

'Yes.'

Jack looked at her solidly and slowly screwed up his eyes for effect.

'But you don't live here, Phil,' he said.

Phil stepped defiantly over the threshold and walked passed him.

'That's hardly the point, Jack,' she said over-defensively. 'If we all looked after our own little patch what a selfish place the world would be. Now where's my granddaughter?'

She was already on her way down the stairs. Jack smiled, and watched as she repeated her limp, but rather glorious, excuse to Margaret.

Amy sat in a small café by King's Cross, turning her finger around in the sugar bowl, reading the menu again. She had sat there for an hour nursing what the fat, grease-stained, proprietor advertised as cappuccino. Perhaps she'd chosen this café almost wilfully. It was the sort of place people waited in for the late night buses. Now it was mid-evening and its clientele were a mix of taxi drivers, a couple of punks, and an old woman who looked as if she'd escaped here from a little bedsit that she couldn't afford to heat.

A miserable drizzle collected on the wire-reinforced window pane and ran slowly down in worm-like trails. On the radio they were announcing the afternoon's football results. To Amy it sounded an interminable litany, even the single figure scores gave a meanness to this game.

She watched the old woman tutting to herself, and the young punk staring blankly into a cup of tea. Hardly the image of teenage rebellion.

Perhaps she'd come in here to punish herself, she thought, a punishment for thinking it would be easy to throw up a job, leave Susan and Alain to it, and set herself up as Mary Poppins.

Margaret had busied herself with 'attacking' the kitchen. It wasn't just that 'the American girl you insisted on' had reduced it to chaos in a single week, but that it was a kitchen 'without any clear direction'. By this she meant that things were in the wrong cupboards. Jack was determined not to interpret this as a major personal failing. That tinned foods could be stored lower, and separate from packets and dried food, had never really crossed his field of experience. He was sure it hadn't troubled Sarah too much either. There was sense, of course, in his mother's assertion that saucepans, ideally, should not be stored in the higher cupboards. They tended to fall out and strike you a nasty blow on the head.

After Margaret had pulled the entire contents of the cupboards out, and marshalled them all, like battalions, she refilled the cupboards with military precision.

Then she turned her attention to the freezer chest, the depths of which were a mystery to Jack.

Michael and Jack were watching rugby on the tele-vision. Jack tended to shout a great deal, and run up to the screen, and hold his head in his hands when the rugby was on. His father sat quiet, and intently still, occasionally grunting. As spectators of the game they may as well have been at opposite ends of the pitch.

'Jack . . .' called Margaret 'can you come and have a look at some of this lamb.'

He went into the laundry room where she had removed certain items from the freezer chest.

'This leg of lamb, dear, you might want to toss it out, it says on the label "eat by May".' She handed him the leg of lamb. It was part of the batch that the removal men had dumped in the chest. He looked at the label.

It was Sarah's handwriting. A flowing, calligraphic script in black ink, with one of her little squiggles beneath that she sometimes signed little notes to him with.

He held the freezing lamb in his hands and stared at it, gradually squeezing it harder. He read the note over and over again. Eat by May. She must have written it back in December. He could feel his heart thumping, and his hands began to hurt with the frost.

What sort of dinner party would Sarah have made of it? he wondered. He couldn't possibly eat it without her.

He replaced it slowly into the chest. He couldn't throw it out either, to decompose in the bin. It was banal, in many ways, he knew, to feel so deeply about a damned leg of lamb.

Margaret looked confused and stared again at the label. Slowly it began to dawn on her. She touched her son's arm. He shook his head and smiled thinly. He went back to the rugby. His father was standing in front of the screen, spitting expletives.

Jack sat silently on the sofa.

Amy came back at nine. Margaret, Michael and Phil were long gone. He listened as she let herself in and began walking up the stairs.

Jack jumped up. She was obviously heading straight for her room, keeping out of his way.

'Hello' he called.

She turned on the stair. 'Hi.'

'All right?' asked Jack, awkwardly.

Fine, thanks,' she said, and went to walk on.

'Have you eaten?' he said, as brightly as he could.

'Yes.'

He gave her one of his schoolboy smiles.

'Well come and have a drink then?' he said.

'I won't.'

This was awful, he'd created an 'atmosphere', as his mother would term it.

'No, come on,' he insisted. 'The baby's down. It'd be nice.'

So English, thought Amy, 'It'd be nice . . .' She followed him downstairs.

'How was your day?' she asked.

Jack sniggered. 'We were invaded. What did you get up to?'

Amy chewed her lip. 'Not a lot. Went to see some friends. Saw some of the sights, movie, went for a meal. Nothing special.'

She hovered in the kitchen, looking around her. She was sure something had changed. All the utensils seemed to have been moved by a sorcerer's apprentice. Jack got a bottle of wine from the fridge.

Perhaps things wouldn't be so bad, he obviously didn't actually want her to become invisible every time he was in the house. She went to get two wine glasses.

The doorbell rang.

'I don't believe it!' yelled Jack.

Amy smiled. 'I'll get it' she said.

On the doorstep was a rather glamorous young woman holding a bottle of champagne.

Jack looked up in surprise as they came down the stairs.

'I knew you'd be stuck in with the infant so I thought I'd pop over with a bottle to cheer you up,' said Anna.

'Well, this is a surprise,' said Jack.

Amy reached for another wine glass and made her way across the room with all three. As she passed Anna, Anna caught her by the elbow and deftly took two of the glasses. She looked down at the remaining one in Amy's hand. Her eyes seemed to suddenly flare. Then she smiled at her coldly, and through gritted teeth said: 'Goodnight.'

Amy laid down her empty. It was just incredible how rude the English could be sometimes. She was so amazed that she simply muttered a quick 'good night' and went up to her room.

18

Amy spent the first part of Sunday morning religiously telephoning landlords.

Jack was relieved. From the outset he hadn't intended that she should live in. It could never work for him. He needed a nanny but he certainly didn't need a lodger or a flatmate. He was glad when she set off on her trawl around Islington.

'Best of luck, hope you find somewhere nice,' he called as she left the house.

'Sure,' she called optimistically, and skipped out of the door. She'd selected six places to see.

Jack smiled, breathed a sigh of relief, and took Sarah upstairs for a long soapy bath.

Only an hour later the front door opened again. He listened as her footsteps thudded miserably down the stairs to where he was playing with Sarah in the kitchen room.

They were all asking the most outrageous rents, she said, it was just impossible. She hung her head hopelessly. Then she picked up a colour supplement and turned to the fashion pages.

Jack found a copy of the *Evening Standard* and a copy of *Time Out* and began thumbing through the rental columns until he found somewhere that was acceptable to her price-wise. It was a studio flat with a kitchen diner, just a little way across town in King's Cross. There was an excellent tube link, and it was situated in an 'historic and dignified' Victorian street. Jack offered to drive her over there straight away.

Jack, Amy and Sarah got into the car.

They drew up outside a large old Victorian house that had been converted into flats.

'Is this it then?' said Jack.

Amy looked at the scrap of paper on her lap that Jack had scribbled the address on.

'Yes, this is it,' she said, quietly.

Jack turned to look at the building again. There was no doubt that it had once been a dignified Victorian house, it was a little faded now, but possibly still very nice inside. He wondered what had really happened to make her leave her friend Susan's warehouse, especially because they still seemed to be best friends.

A length of guttering flapped from the cornice in the wind. Someone had sprayed an anarchist logo on the peeling paintwork, a lively colourful area, King's Cross. But if buildings can be said to have expressions then this had that of a dirty old man loitering in a dimly-lit alleyway.

Where there were curtains at the windows they were in tatters of dirty oranges and purples. Jack began to have severe doubts.

'Are you sure this is the address?' he said.

She checked the paper again.

'Yes,' she said, nodding and looking up at the building with a resolute expression on her face.

She'd talked to the landlord on the telephone. 'Did he say what it was like inside?' asked Jack.

'No, but it can't be any worse than the others I've seen today.'

'Look, there's no rush, you know. I didn't mean to rush you out or anything.'

'No, I know,' she said and flashed him a quick conciliatory smile. Her clothes were still hung from the window frame because she hadn't liked to intrude on his wife's things. Perhaps it would be more fun to have her own place.

They got out of the car, Amy holding Sarah. They walked up the steps to the door. There must have been a dozen doorbells, tacked and Sellotaped to the doorframe, where the screws had failed. The bells spoke of an odd selection of tenants. Their names were written in ancient and faded Biro. Some of them just gave initials. One, more ominously, merely said: 'Top Floor – Cindy'.

Amy pressed the doorbell to the first-floor flat. They waited for some time, then they heard a thumping down the stairs, and a call of, 'all right, all right . . .'

The door cracked open to reveal a middle-aged man in a vest, thick glasses, and sinister, prurient eyes, that were accentuated by bushy eyebrows gleaming with some sort of oil he'd used on his remaining hair.

'You the one after the ad?' he demanded brusquely.

'That's right,' said Amy, 'I called a while ago.'

The man looked at Sarah in her arms. He screwed up his face in revulsion.

'No dogs, no babies, don't care what you do with men,' he said, flashing an equally revolted glance at Jack.

'Pleased to hear it,' said Amy, dryly.

'Oh no,' said Jack, 'this isn't for the baby and me, I've just driven Amy over. It's just one person.'

'Well as I said,' grumbled the man, and he turned back into the hallway and began walking towards a flight of stairs. They presumed they were meant to follow him.

There was a dank smell to the house that Jack hadn't experienced since playing in old bomb shelters as a kid. But this wasn't just the smell of long decay, this was more active than that. It was a cocktail of boiled cabbage, rotting furniture and paraffin from lethal heaters.

They climbed the stairs. 'Climb' being, for once, exactly the right word for it. The stairs were uneven. The banister rail was sticky to the touch. Jack felt as if he was mounting the gallows. Amy's expression was fixed. One of resolved acceptance.

The landlord was making some sort of speech. Reeling it off by rote: 'Hundred a week including service charge. Four weeks up front. Four weeks' notice. Cash, no cheques, no delays, no excuses and we'll all be happy.'

The phrase 'we'll all be happy' echoed against the filthy wallpaper. Wallpaper that looked as though it had been there since the fifties, rubbed almost entirely away by the transients who'd passed through, moving quickly up this flight to their horrid little beds.

Surely, thought Jack, people don't still rent out places like this?

They got to a door on the third floor. There were screw holes in the wood where former locks had been wrenched off. The man unlocked it and pushed. At first the door wouldn't open at all, and Jack was sure there'd be a body slumped behind it. Finally it shuddered open in starts. Jack noticed the thick wedge of black dirt beneath the landlord's fingernails as he reached for the lightswitch. A lightswitch which clung to the wall with a circle of finger printed grime around it.

Amy was trying to take in as little of it as possible. She wasn't a person with much choice in this city, right now, she thought.

The only good thing that could possibly be said about the room was that it was small. Any larger and God knows what other atrocities it would have contained. It was one of those horrible bedsits where everything is patterned in clashing garish colours. The curtains had been designed by someone with a grudge. The carpet had been burned by two hundred cigarettes, and the cigarettes had been right. The pattern seemed to want, with all its jagged swirls, to bite at your feet.

The single bed was against a wall, and lay there stark and bare. The wardrobe was ancient with a cracked mirror on its door. The stretch covers on the modest armchair had, well, stretched. These were the three elements of the room that allowed it, by law, to be described as 'furnished'.

'I thought you said it had a kitchen?' said Amy.

The man gave a bored grunt and walked over to where a bit of orange curtaining, with splatters of ketchup, hung from a piece of wire that was stretched diagonally across the corner of the room. He pulled it back. Behind was a sink, a Baby Belling electric oven, a battered kettle and a bucket.

Jack looked at Amy.

She shrugged her shoulders.

'Well I wasn't planning any large dinner parties,' she said, bravely.

'And where's the bathroom?' said Jack.

He was now almost fascinated by how appalling this landlord could be. It was like peeling an onion to discover that every layer was more rotten than the last.

'Next floor' he said, gruffly, as if it was obvious that it would be. Jack left Amy and went up to inspect it.

It was a dark foreboding door indeed. Jack pushed it open.

A young guy, spotty and unshaven, sick around the eyes, and obviously stoned, sat with his trousers around his ankles. He looked slowly up from the lavatory. Jack was frozen to the spot in the doorway. The young man brightened a little as he looked up at Jack. His staring, dead, eyes fixed on him.

'Got any bog roll, man?' he said. He was ready to befriend Jack for a couple of sheets. Jack slammed the door shut.

He went back to the bedsit. Amy was counting out notes for her deposit.

'You're not staying here,' he said.

'Jack . . .' said Amy. There was a cold, grey, pain in her eyes, but a certain amount of admirable fortitude as well.

'Come on,' said Jack, leading her by the arm. 'And get Sarah outside before she catches something.'

'Now wait a minute . . .' said the landlord, suddenly ferociously indignant.

Jack put his hand up in front of him. 'Now please don't say anything. I hate getting aggressive. I'm not very good at it and it upsets me for the rest of the day. Amy, come on.'

Jack was almost shaking with fury as he picked up Amy's bags and marched out, taking the stairs two at a time until he got to the street.

Amy came out after him.

'Jack, what are you doing?'

'We can find you something better than that,' he said.

Amy leaned against the railings of the building.

'Oh can we? I've looked. This is London. That's all I can afford.'

'Well then . . . well then . . .' he said, realising that he was about to offer the solution that had been the furthest from his mind, '. . . then you'll just have to stay with us. This is stupid. It's a waste of time and it'll be a waste of money.' He smiled at her. There, he'd done it. He'd relented. She could share his home.

Her eyes narrowed. 'Oh no,' she said. 'I'm not staying with you. I've had it.'

'What? Why not?' How could she possibly reject his home for this?

'I just don't want to, that's all.' A slight note of petulance in her voice.

Jack was amazed.

'Why?'

She swallowed hard, and began, 'Because I've had it, that's why. I've just had it. I'm tired of the constant criticism during the week and pissed off with sitting around in my room all evening pretending I'm not there. I'm not a servant . . .'

Jack was shocked.

'No one said you were.'

'Then don't treat me like one. It's so fucking English.'

'I don't,' said Jack, beginning to sound petulant himself.

'You do. You all do. I didn't even want this job in the first place. I didn't ask for it. You asked me. I don't even know why I'm doing it. I must be crazy. I was perfectly happy being miserable.'

She made a move to grab her bags.

'Amy . . .'

'The only one who's nice to me,' she continued 'is Sarah. And she's a baby, for God's sake. She doesn't know any better.'

She turned back towards the house. Jack was speech-less, but he knew he had to retrieve the situation quickly.

'I apologise . . .' he blurted. 'OK? I'm sorry, genuinely, deeply sorry, all right?'

She turned back to him and faced him expressionlessly.

'I apologise,' he said again. 'You'll stay?'

The landlord had appeared at the doorway and slammed it shut.

'I'll think about it,' said Amy.

'Fine. Good. It's settled then.'

He took her bags and put them in the boot of the car.

He was immediately bright again, like a small child that bawls at one moment and laughs the next. Like a child that forgets his misdemeanour the moment the punishment is administered.

'It'll mean a pay cut, of course, now I know what accommodation is worth.'

'What?' said Amy, taken aback.

He took Sarah from her.

'We're going to Camden Lock Market today. You coming?'

He opened the car door for her. She got in.

Was this really an invitation to spend Sacred Sunday with Sarah and him? Obviously it was.

They drove to Camden. Jack was quite jolly. A weight had been lifted from him. He'd done something decent. Now they just had to make it work.

It's a big enough house, Jack was thinking, and it is entirely unreasonable for me to object to her so much, simply because she's not Sarah's mother.

He thought for a moment of that nanny that had laughed like a horse. His daughter could have done a lot worse than Amy. There was something of the baby, the vulnerable infant, about her too. And it was already apparent that Sarah liked Amy, responded to her, and Amy had become immediately fond of Sarah.

He could no more see her live in that squalid bedsit in King's Cross, or its cheaper equivalent in Tufnell Park, or Seven Sisters, which had been next on his list, than he would entrust little Sarah to Miss Starch Knickers.

Jack wondered who Amy was really. Why she'd come to London to lead this sort of life.

Amy glanced at Jack as he drove through the London traffic. He appeared to be in command of this town. He knew the short cuts, the stores, was at ease with it as a capital. But he was not at ease with himself, she could see that.

She worried for a moment, what did he want from her, why were they going to Camden Market? She had spent the last week treading on eggshells, and every eggshell was a memory of Sarah. Her spectre loomed so large sometimes she expected to meet Mrs Danvers on the stairs.

They walked through the market, Jack with his baby strapped to his chest. It was odd the way people smiled at them. Of course, thought Amy, they think we're a couple. Married even. The odd thing about it was that it didn't disturb her. Strangers saw them as a unit and there was something quite nice about that. Something essentially reassuring, even if it was only an illusion.

Jack was fascinated by the stalls. It was years since he'd been here, and then it was only briefly. Sarah and he had never bothered with it. It was a rotten drive from Hammersmith and when they'd planned to go on a Sunday they'd always thrown an improvised lunch instead and got too tiddled to make it. Amy had never made it to Camden Lock either and she was really quite surprised and intrigued by it. It was a good feeling to be in the middle of a bustle, rubbing shoulders with all sorts.

They stopped to watch the jugglers and the fire eaters, and a girl who made the most enormous bubbles by dipping a coat hanger into a washing up bowl. They were delighted by the displays. Painted kites. Papier mâché creatures. Candlesticks. There was an innocence about the artefacts that made the market a little oasis of whimsy and eccentricity in the centre of this dirty brutal city. The music of folk songs, Andean pan pipes, filled the air. It was the perfect antidote to that tawdry bedsit they'd escaped in King's Cross.

Jack bought a little mirror, with a swirling painted surround of starfish and sea horses that Amy had admired.

'Here you are,' he said. 'You did like it, didn't you? You can put it up in your room.' They laughed.

'My room!' said Amy, as if she were mentally taking possession of it.

'You can call it a 'room warming' present!'

They crossed the bridge over the canal, and came to a stall selling hats. Amy tried on a pudding basin of a thing made from velvet. Then Jack saw the ones that were made for babies. He laughed.

'Look at this fucking silly hat' he said. It was an angular Peruvian thing with llamas on it, and a little bell that tinkled.

'I know,' said Amy, 'wouldn't it suit her so perfectly?'

'It would,' said Jack. 'As long as my mother never saw her in it.'

Amy went suddenly quiet. Jack laughed again.

'It's OK' he said, 'it's not part of the job to get along with my mother.'

'Thank God. She makes me nervous,' said Amy.

'She makes everyone nervous! Don't worry about it. She means well, it just comes out wrong sometimes.'

She smiled. 'Let me buy the hat,' she said.

He was touched. 'You don't have to do that,' he said.

She picked the hat from the stall. 'I want to,' she said and turned to the pale-faced girl, with a ring through her nose, who was serving. 'I'll take it, thanks.'

She slid it on Sarah's head and they walked on, touring the stalls, tinkling.

'She does look great in that hat, doesn't she?'

'She sure does,' said Amy, 'smells bad, though.' It did – it smelled of goats.

'Let's have something to eat,' said Jack, 'you must be starving.' They stopped at a stall selling huge slices of deep pan pizza and went to sit on a bench by the canal.

'There's no polite way to eat these,' said Jack as the mozzarella strung through his teeth.

'That's OK, you're with an American . . .'

'I am,' he said, and they smiled at each other happily for a moment as the pizza dripped from their lips.

'I'm really enjoying myself,' said Amy, 'I guess you have to see London with a Londoner. I saw nothing but Susan's warehouse and the restaurant . . .'

They watched the people passing. The young punks with their moment of purple hair and rebellion. The old trendies in their corduroy. The young professionals clutching their spoils: cast iron Victorian fire surrounds, terracotta pots, bags of brass door handles. All of them, as they passed, turned to look at the baby, and then up at Jack and Amy to smile.

It was oddly elemental, as if people wanted to touch the baby for luck. The older people, the middle-aged women especially, stopped and cooed. It was as if they were trying to touch something of their own early mother-hood, through Amy.

Two men, both in their forties, stopped. They were dressed identically in denim, with outrageous moustaches and one of them had a toy poodle on a lead with a ruby-studded collar.

'Love the hat! Isn't it gorge?' he said.

'I couldn't see you in it!' said the other, cattily, but they still smiled broadly at the 'couple' with their baby. The poodle began sniffing at Jack's shoe.

'Jasper!' said the guy, tugging him back, and turning to Jack. 'He's obsessed with feet,' he said rather campily. 'Give him a chance and he'll have your leg off.' He turned to the baby. 'Is yours teething yet?'

'No, not yet,' said Jack, with a wry smirk.

'You've all that to come, then,' said the other to Amy, with a great sigh of feigned experience. The little poodle began yapping. 'Oh, come on you!' said the guy, picking up the dog, 'Don't start a scene!' They went on their way.

An elderly woman in an ancient astrakhan coat stopped to talk.

'Oh, doesn't he look a picture?' she said, stroking Sarah under the chin.

When she'd gone Amy turned to Jack. 'Why does everyone think she's a boy?' she asked.

Jack sniggered. 'Don't worry about it, when she's got more hair . . .'

They went home, went downstairs to the kitchen room and opened a bottle of white wine. Jack picked up two glasses and brought them over. They flopped on to the sofa and for the first time began to relax in each other's company. Maybe this would be workable after all, he thought.

They'd had a pleasant afternoon, but Sarah was tired. They took her up to bed together. The fresh air, the jogging through the market, maybe even the Peruvian hat had somehow exhausted the little girl. Jack laid her in her crib and kissed her on the forehead.

They watched a movie on TV, Jack even laughed at the odd joke in it. They both yawned at the same time. It was time for bed for them too. On their way up they looked in on Sarah. She was sleeping soundly, her tiny fingers curled up on the pillow beside her face. She had a cheeky little expression even when she was asleep.

'She's so good. Such a good baby,' said Amy.

'Yeah,' said Jack. 'I don't know where it comes from. Must be her mother's genes, certainly not mine'.

Amy was leaning over Sarah's crib, her smooth, perfect skin, and her sparkling eyes, so like little Sarah's in many ways.

'I guess we ought to go to bed,' said Jack, finally breaking the silence.

They nodded at each other. Smiling as they went to part on the landing.

'It's been a wonderful day. Thank you' she said. 'I've really enjoyed myself.'

'Me too,' said Jack, 'great fun.'

'Thank you,' said Amy again, as she turned towards her room, feeling for the first time that it was her room. 'Goodnight' she said slowly. They stared at each other.

'Goodnight,' said Jack.

They stood where they were for a moment longer.

Then they each took themselves off to their separate rooms. Both of them wondering if it had nearly been otherwise. It would have been a mistake, of course. Of course it would have been . . .

19

Monday morning. Jack was on the verge of leaving for work, stretching out his last minutes in the house as far as possible. The doorbell rang and, presuming it was probably William, he ran to the door.

It was Alain, the owner of the brasserie who had fired Amy. The man looked rather surprised to see Jack. He was evidently expecting Amy to answer the door.

'Hi . . .' he said awkwardly. 'Is, um . . . is Amy here?'

Jack thought for a moment. Had he come to take her back? He couldn't imagine, for a moment, that this man was capable of an apology. Either to Amy or him.

'Yes she is. Um, come in,' he said. He was rather intrigued. Amy was such a mystery, maybe this was the next episode in the serial of her life.

He led Alain downstairs.

Amy was standing beside the sink. Alain was startled to see that she was wearing just a T-shirt. The one she slept in. Amy turned around and stared at him nervously, flashing a short, sharp, glare at Jack. Perhaps he shouldn't have let him in. That's what she seemed to be signalling.

Amy didn't say a word but stood waiting for Alain to speak. He didn't know where to begin and was floundering.

Jack performed a quick little mime, which was totally

unintelligible to them. He jumped on the spot for a moment doing an odd little hand jive. It was meant to indicate that he needed to polish his shoes and he scuttled out into the utility room.

'I brought your tips,' said Alain at last.

Amy said nothing. There was a cold critical stare on his face as he looked her up and down in her T-shirt. He was on dangerous ground, he knew, but he said it anyway: 'Do you always walk around here dressed like that?'

Amy was furious.

'Mostly,' she said '. . . except for when I walk around naked.'

'You practically are naked,' he snapped. 'Are you sleeping with him?'

Jack was slipping on his shoes as quietly as possible so that he could listen. 'Will you keep your voice down?' he heard her say.

'Just answer the question,' he was saying.

'No,' she said. 'It's none of your goddammed business.'

An evil smile came over his face as his jealousy burned like acid.

'So you are!' he said, as if he'd achieved some sort of triumph. 'I knew it.'

'I didn't say that.'

'You didn't give me a chance.'

'All right then,' he said, imagining this to be reasonable behaviour. 'Are you sleeping with him?'

Jack had his shoes on, but hovered in the utility room, enjoying every minute of it.

'Well, are you?' persisted Alain.

Amy was now getting very cross. 'What if I am?'

'Christ, you've only been here a week,' Alain said.

'Didn't take you that long,' she said dismissively.

'That's got nothing to do with it.' He floundered again. This part of the inquisition had run its natural course.

'Why've you come here?'

'I told you. I brought your tips.'

'So leave them on the side and go.'

Jack came back into the room, snatching up his briefcase, a mischievous grin in his eye. He swept up to Amy.

'I'm late,' he said. 'What else is new? Thanks for ironing my shirt, sweetheart. I'll see you later.' He slipped his hands around her waist and kissed her on the neck. He looked up to see Alain's face. The Frenchman was nodding.

He was furious.

'If you've finished I'll show you out,' said Jack, curtly.

'Of course,' he said.

Jack marched him up the stairs and out of the front door. The man seemed to have more to say but couldn't possibly phrase it. Jack came to a halt on the top step.

'Shit,' he said. 'Forgot my keys. Nice to see you again.' He darted back into the house and shut the door behind Alain, leaving him bemused on the doorstep.

Jack, of course, hadn't forgotten his keys at all. He came skipping back down the stairs to Amy, pleased as punch with himself.

'Well, that got rid of him!'

She was silent. Silently fuming.

'What?' he said.

'Why did you do that?' She was upset.

'Did you see his face?'

'Who the hell do you think you are?' she said, picking up Sarah and walking out of the room.

Jack stood for a moment. What had he done now, where had he gone wrong?

He took himself off to work.

Jack was a little confused. It had been a while since he'd given one of his 'performances', and found it very confusing that it had so horribly backfired. It was especially disappointing because he'd woken up with a warm feeling from how well the weekend had gone. He'd felt quite the knight in shining armour. Now it had all fallen so quickly to pieces again.

He stared into the florist's next to WW&P. Flowers! he thought. Send some flowers round and that'll patch it all up. He walked in and chose a selection. Tiger lilies, anemones, sweet williams, a stem of twisted willow. He began to write on a card. He swirled the pen above it. What does one say? He handed the card back.

'No, no message,' he said. He gave them his address, paid, and made to leave the shop.

'Anna!' he said. She stared at him inquisitively.

'Hello . . .' she said, and waited.

'Mother's birthday . . .' he said.

'Ah . . .' A feeble explanation.

'And you?'

'Me?' said Anna, confidently. A person with nothing to hide in a florist's shop.

'It's Monday. I always buy flowers for myself on a Monday.'

'Really?'

'Yes, really. It's a thing I do.'

He looked at her curiously. Perhaps she meant she bought them for the office.

*

Jack called home mid-morning. The line was engaged.

Amy was telephoning her mother. She had the receiver under her chin, and a screaming Sarah in her arms.

'She won't stop,' she was saying. 'Whatever I do. I'm sure it's her teeth or something . . . valium!? You didn't give me valium. Are you serious . . .? What do you mean, just a bit of a tablet crushed up in my milk . . .? God, Mom, that's terrible. I could've been in rehab before I was in kindergarten . . . yes . . . yes, I'm sure it worked. Listen I gotta go. Go back to sleep. I'll talk to you later.'

She sat on the sofa trying to calm Sarah. She wondered if it was because she was churned up over Alain, and Sarah had caught her mood.

Jack got in from work. The flowers he had sent were in a large glass vase on the mantelpiece. They looked stunning. Amy and Sarah were sitting quietly.

'Hello darling,' he said, kissing Sarah. He turned towards the flowers, feigning surprise.

'Oh, they look wonderful,' he said.

'Yeah,' said Amy, flatly, 'they arrived this afternoon.'

Jack smiled.

'He must be really hurting,' she said. Jack was puzzled. The penny dropped. Damn, she thought that bastard Alain had sent them.

'Obviously . . .' he said quietly.

'I would've thrown them out but it seemed a waste.'

'Yes,' said Jack, 'a waste . . .'

20

June, and summer was looking surprisingly promising for England. It was a hot afternoon, with a light breeze, carrying the smell of freshly-mown grass.

Jack, Phil and Pamela stood arm in arm in the churchyard around Sarah's grave which had just had its simple headstone put in place.

Pamela read the inscription that Jack had put on it.

Death lies on her like an untimely frost
Upon the sweetest flower of all the field.

'It's beautiful, Jack,' said Pamela.

'D'you think she would have liked it?'

'Yes,' said Phil. 'She loved your sentimentality.'

Pamela sighed. 'You've written it beautifully,' she said.

'It's Shakespeare,' he said.

'It is,' said Pamela 'it's pure Shakespeare.'

Jack shook his head and smiled. 'No, Pamela, it *is* Shakespeare. *Romeo and Juliet*.' He laughed wickedly at her. No one would believe she was now at Cambridge reading English literature.

He turned to Phil.

'Do you think we should have a little service?'

'No I don't think so. I don't see why we should put ourselves through all that again.'

Jack was silent for a moment. It was perfectly quiet, the football season had ended and the ground was empty. There was just the sound of the breeze in the yew trees and the buzzing of the bees around the flowers they had laid.

'I'm just thinking how odd it is that one day little Sarah will be standing up here looking at me down there.' He sighed.

'Oh don't be so morbid,' said Phil. But she stood and stared at the headstone too.

'Come on,' said Pamela. They turned away and walked toward the bench where Amy was sitting with Sarah.

'So how's Cambridge?' Jack asked.

'Fine. The course is great, and . . .' Pamela began to twinkle.

'And . . .?'

'No. Nothing,' she said, pulling herself up.

'The course is great and "no nothing"?'

Pamela turned her head away.

'I've met someone,' she said.

'You've not! What's his name, what does he do? What's he look like?' said Jack impatiently.

'I'm not telling you. It's none of your business.' She was refusing to be drawn, and rather enjoying it.

Jack stopped on the path. Phil was already at the bench with Amy, cradling Sarah.

He was excited by her news. 'You have to. I need to know who little Pammie's shagging.'

'Oh, Jack, you can be so crude!' she exclaimed, refusing to give him any more details that he would undoubtedly use to torture her.

'Sorry,' he said. 'It was just a joke.'

Pamela glanced towards Amy sitting on the bench. Sunning herself.

'So have you poked the nanny yet?'

'Pamela!' said Jack, outraged.

'Just a joke . . .' she replied, rather pleased with herself. Jack was impressed.

They walked out of the churchyard, Jack and Phil's steps growing slower and slower the nearer they got to the gate. It was a difficult place to leave behind.

21

'This is intolerable!' came William's voice from the utility room. Amy looked up from feeding Sarah.

'Wonder what I've done now,' she said. William walked into the room holding a babysuit that he'd taken out of the washing machine. He was staring at it as if it gave great offence. Then he glowered at Amy.

'Look at this,' he snapped. 'Just look at it. Ruined.'

The babysuit was a heavy shade of streaky purple and grey.

'So it's a bit darker than it was.' Amy shrugged.

'It was white!' exclaimed William.

'Just leave it. I'll do something about it later.'

'No, miss!' he said authoritatively. 'You leave it. This is the fourth of the child's garments you've destroyed in the course of a fortnight. I do the washing. Leave it to me.' He smacked his hands against his apron.

'I look after Sarah's clothes, Bill.'

He winced.

'But you don't! That is precisely my point. I know what you're up to but don't think you'll ever fill her dear mother's shoes because you won't.'

Amy gritted her teeth. Now, that was unfair. She steadied herself. She'd have liked to have said that, for one: Jack's wife had never even got the chance to be Sarah's 'dear mother' and for two: was he such big buddies with her anyway? Wasn't he drunk in the square at that time?

'Just give it here,' she said. Sarah started to cry.

'Leave it!' snapped William.

'I said, give it here.'

'Leave it with me.'

Amy snatched at the babysuit. William held on with a firm grip. They both pulled at it like dogs on the end of a rag. There was a loud rip.

Jack was just coming in from work, and stood on the stairs watching the pathetic tussle. He was furious.

'Sarah is yelling her head off, Amy!' he growled.

Amy went to pick her up, marching silently across the room.

William looked at Jack. A frown stealing across his forehead.

'Nothing's ever ironed properly,' he said, defending himself. 'Sarah's forever creased.'

'It's her responsibility.'

'It's mine!' said William. At any moment he was going to stamp his foot.

'It was yours, now it's hers.'

William was looking petulant. Jack stared at the babysuit, which had been torn in two. What was he supposed to do here? Make a judgement of Solomon?

'She never puts anything away,' continued William. 'Everything's been a mess since she arrived. She's making my job impossible.'

'You're not making hers any easier.'

'I'm sorry but there's a point of principle here,' William said, rising up on the soles of his shoes. 'I either do the washing or I don't. If I'm not allowed to wash the little lady's wardrobe I shall have to consider my position most carefully.' He furrowed his brow for effect.

'Well, if you feel you must,' said Jack.

William didn't alter his expression but he was clearly flabbergasted.

'You can be assured I shall,' he said stiffly, thrusting his shoulders back. Jack walked out of the room leaving William to slap his hands on his apron.

Amy was sulking in the living-room with Sarah.

'I'm sorry about her clothes,' she said, 'but it's not true about the mess and you know that!'

Jack had had an extremely difficult day at work. He sighed heavily.

'William is a nice man and a good friend. We're family to him, Sarah and I, and that's important to me.'

'OK . . . so let him do the washing. It's no big deal really.'

They smiled a little. It was true, it was no big deal, except for the fact that this seemed to have become a very complicated household.

When Jack got in from the office the next evening he could hear the sound of happy splashing from the bathroom.

He bounded up the stairs. He had a yellow fluffy duck under his arm that Jackie, his secretary, had made and he was excited about giving it to Sarah.

'Hello,' he called, taking the stairs two at a time.

'We're in the bath,' came Amy's voice.

He poked the head of the fluffy duck around the bathroom door, gave out a Donald Duck 'hello', and leapt into the bathroom.

He stopped dead. Amy was wet and naked too. He jumped back out on to the landing.

'God! I didn't realise you meant we . . . I thought you just meant "we",' he said, flustered at having burst in on her in the bath.

Amy wasn't flustered about it at all. She wasn't even conscious of this kind of English reserve. 'You don't mind do you?' she said innocently, thinking the mistake was hers.

'No, no. Not at all,' said Jack, opening his eyes again, embarrassed. 'No, that's great . . .' he said, splashing about himself, but for words. 'Listen, are you doing anything tonight?' he asked.

'No, I'm not. Why?' she said, intrigued.

'It's just that I've been asked out, that's all. It's not important, so if you've got something lined up . . .'

It obviously was important, he couldn't hide the tone in his voice.

Amy had already imagined the pair of them taking in a movie, or a meal.

'No, nothing' she said. 'You go out. Have a great time.'

'You sure?'

'Yeah, sure.' She looked towards the door, curious. 'Who's it with?' she said, casually.

'Oh, Anna . . .' he said, as quickly and dismissively as possible. There was silence from inside the bathroom.

Amy looked at Sarah, and putting two fingers in her mouth, mimed gagging at the sound of Anna's name. The little baby followed suit. Amy laughed.

'That'll be . . . nice,' she said.

Jack changed his clothes. Anna and he were going to see a play that Phil had recommended. It seemed an age since he'd been to anything so public as a play. Since Sarah's death he'd been entirely unable to suspend his disbelief long enough to suffer a fiction or a film.

*

They met up at a wine bar in Soho. Anna already had a bottle of champagne on ice at a corner table.

Since he'd last seen her in the office she had, quite literally, let her hair down. She was wearing a cocktail dress, and looked altogether less severe than she did at work. Over the last couple of weeks they'd taken to having the 'odd glass' together after work, and they had really started to become very easy in each other's company.

Anna kissed him on the lips.

'I thought for a moment you were going to stand me up,' she said.

'Why?'

'Oh, I just thought perhaps once you got home, and got "involved", you wouldn't want to come out again.'

'No, no. Everything's fine at home.'

'Hostilities have died down between the butler and the governess?'

Jack laughed, embarrassed.

'So how is your American girl settling in?'

Jack took a gulp of his champagne, slightly amused that she spoke of Amy in much the way that his mother did. Hostilities hadn't abated on that front.

'She'll be fine. She keeps herself to herself,' he said. 'Stays in her room, mainly, reading blockbusters,' he said, lying thinly.

They gossiped about the scandals and intrigues of the office until it was time to dash down Shaftsbury Avenue for the play. They slipped into their seats as the lights were going down.

During the play Jack watched a couple two rows in front. They were obviously on a first date. Every time the man turned to whisper a comment in her ear she responded with giggles she could barely stifle. When the guy laughed at a joke in the play he took the opportunity to move his arm to the back of her seat.

Jack, amused, pointed it out to Anna. She laughed, losing for a moment her usual rigid composure. Jack put his arm around the back of her seat.

The play ended and they stepped out into the neon glare of Shaftesbury Avenue. Anna took his arm. Suddenly he heard a familiar voice in the crowd.

'Jack!'

They turned around. There was Margaret, Michael beside her. 'What a surprise!' she said, knowing that Phil would have recommended the play to him too, but she wasn't really looking at Jack. Her eyes were fixed on Anna. Jack slowly slipped his arm back to his side.

'Mother . . . Dad, you remember Anna. From work . . . the managing partner.'

Margaret's eyes lit up instantly, and she beamed. It was like watching them switch on the Christmas lights on Regent Street.

'Of course I do. How are you?' she said.

'Fine, thank you,' said Anna.

Margaret simply stood there beaming benignly while Michael shuffled from foot to foot embarrassed once again by how transparent his wife could be.

'Did you enjoy the play?' he asked.

'No, I didn't' said Anna with a smile.

Margaret smiled even wider. 'Oh good,' she said. 'Neither did I.' Margaret thoroughly enjoyed disliking new plays. That was the whole purpose in going to see them. She considered herself a faultless theatre critic: she hated everything equally. But she certainly approved of Anna.

188

'You two must come round for dinner,' she said, shamelessly cataloguing them as a couple. Jack could barely look her in the eye.

'That'd be wonderful,' said Anna.

'D'you play bridge?' asked Margaret.

'I do,' Anna said.

There was a pause. Until now it hadn't seemed possible that Margaret could smile any broader. But she could. 'Excellent,' she said.

They bid each other their goodnights and Margaret and Michael walked to their car.

There was a definite skip in Margaret's step.

'You're so transparent sometimes,' said Michael.

'Think of the combined incomes. It's enough to make you faint,' she said and waited while he opened the car door for her. Nothing could detract from her triumph.

Jack stopped his car outside Anna's house.

'Are you sure you won't come in?' asked Anna.

'I won't. Thank you.'

They looked at each other for a moment and then Anna put her hand on his arm.

'Look, I know it's not easy for you, but you really should relax. There's nothing wrong in what we're doing, nothing wrong in what you feel. I find you very attractive, Jack. I want to go to bed with you and I don't see anything wrong in that. But I'm perfectly happy to wait.' With this she kissed him on the cheek, opened the car door, and jumped out.

Jack was confused. It was, in some ways, as if she'd outlined an agenda. This woman who bought herself flowers. She was terribly sexy, and nowhere near as complicated, perhaps, as all the other people in his life. The bridge worried him, though.

He sat miserably in his kitchen, sipping a glass of whisky. Even though he hadn't been to bed with Anna, he'd thought about it. And it appalled and horrified him. It wasn't so much the absurd feeling of infidelity as a recognition, again, that Sarah really had gone and wasn't coming back. And there was the sadness, too, that life does indeed go on.

He seemed to be being pulled in so many directions at the same time. He didn't go to bed until he'd got himself sufficiently deadened by the Jameson's.

22

There was a late summer rush on at the register office across the road from the law offices. Jack was staring out of the window at the guests. The bride was tall and the groom was short, and you could easily see which guests belonged to which family.

He was glad of the distraction. He tried to think of his own marriage happily, and remember the good times that they had had together. It wasn't easy, but he was determined to try his best.

His head was banging fearsomely from the effect of last night's whisky and he was mentally bracing himself for the day ahead. As if secretaries have a second sense about hangovers, Jackie burst in through the door with his mail, clumping her way towards him with a horrible frown.

She slammed it all down on the desk.

'These are this morning's. These are the ones you didn't sign last night. And these are your internals . . .' she said brusquely, with a scowl.

'Any chance of a coffee?' he said, in his most pleading, pathetic voice, that always won everyone over.

'No,' she said and spun on her sling-backs, making for the door.

'Oh good . . .' he muttered, resigning himself to to a day in her bad books.

But when Jackie got to the door she stopped and

turned, laying her hand on the frame. She glowered at him for a few moments and then spoke what was on here mind. 'You know what really bugs me?' she said. 'You're an attractive man. Loads of women'd find you attractive. You could do a lot better than that sour-faced old trout.' With this she marched off across the pile carpet of the corridor.

'Jackie ... Jackie!' he called after her. She didn't return. Even the office was beginning to get like his home.

Just a few minutes later Rob appeared in his office doorway with Gerald standing behind him. Gerald worked with Rob in Divorce.

They had silly smiles on their faces.

'Could we have a moment?' said Rob.

'Yes, of course. What is it?' He hoped it wasn't anything too involved.

'There's something we need to talk about, or rather, something we feel we need to know.'

'Have a right to know, in fact,' said Gerald, smirking suggestively.

'Yes ...?'

Rob stepped into his office. 'There's no way of putting this delicately, really,' he said.

His two colleagues looked out through the glass partition of his office to where Anna was talking to her secretary. Gerald began to snigger. Jack slowly reached for a large hardbound book from his shelf, and with a masterly overarm threw it at Rob, yelling: 'Out ... get out!'

Rob ducked in his doorway, laughing. 'Well, did you?' he yelled.

'Out!'

Rob retreated to the corridor and Jack threw another book. 'Is that a yes or a no?'

Jack shook his head in disbelief. Rob's head came back around the door. His hand up in front of him to shield him from any more missiles. Like the entire *Law Of England*.

'Would it make any difference if I told you I had money on this?'

Jack walked to his office door and slammed it shut.

He spent the week 'keeping his head down' and avoiding them. He also took to having a drink with Anna, in a little discreet wine bar away from the office, after work. On the Wednesday he got home late, nine-thirty, or so. Amy was standing at the ironing board, attacking one of his shirts, and taking furious swigs at a mug of coffee.

'Hi. Sorry I'm late. I should've called,' he said. He was wavering slightly, with an idiotic half-smile on his face.

Amy looked slowly up at him. 'Don't worry. I'm getting used to it.'

'Went out for a quick drink,' he said.

'With Anna?'

'Yes. As it happens.' He rounded on her defensively.

'Just asking.' She laid his shirt aside. 'Your mother called. Wanted to know if you and Anna could go round for lunch on Sunday.'

Jack went to the fridge for a bottle of wine. He began pouring himself a glass.

'What's all this "Anna and me" all of a sudden?'

'I'm just relaying a message,' said Amy.

She reached for another shirt.

'What are you doing?'

'Ironing your shirts . . . William didn't show up today. I'm sorry. It's my fault.'

Jack took a great slug at his wine and slammed the glass down, almost cracking its stem.

'Why's everything so fucking complicated? It was never this complicated before!'

Amy thumped the iron down on to the linen and continued to work in silence. Jack slumped on to the sofa with his bottle.

The following day Jack took the unprecedented step of telephoning his father.

Michael answered.

'It's Thursday,' his father said straight off, 'your mother's at bridge.'

'I know,' said Jack.

'Is it something urgent?' His father was confused, why would Jack be calling him?

'I wondered if I might ask your advice about something,' Jack said. There was silence on the end of the phone.

On Saturday morning Jack drove round to his parents' house and his father got into the car. Jack drove them to Primrose Hill where they parked and got out.

Even though it was summer there was a bracing wind from the east. Twenty or thirty people were out on the hill with their dogs, off their leashes. The dogs bounded past them, as they climbed the hill in silence.

All of London was laid out below them. St Paul's, the river, the Nat West tower in the City. It was as if they were climbing above the whole damn mess of life down there.

They walked doggedly up the hill in their overcoats. Every now and then Michael glanced across at his son, wondering what this summons was for, but Jack was staring fixedly at the path. There was something empty about his eyes and he constantly looked down at the path.

It began to drizzle, but Jack seemed unaware of it. In the strong wind the little drops were really quite sharp on their faces, and hurt. The view of the city below was soon obliterated by a cold, dank, haze.

Finally Jack spoke.

'I'm fucked up, Dad,' he said. 'Completely fucked.' He blurted it out as if there was no other way he could express. His father waited for him to continue. But there was no more his son could say.

'Have you talked to anyone?' asked Michael.

'No.'

His father cleared his throat.

'Would you like me to fix something up? Caroline's very good. She might be helpful,' he said.

'No,' said Jack, in disappointment. And they walked to the top of the hill in a further silence. Then Jack turned towards his father, and held him in his eyes.

'I want to talk to you . . .' he said, and laughed nervously. 'Would that be all right?'

Michael looked at his son. He looked so desperate, like someone adrift in freezing seas, looking for any piece of wreckage to cling on to. But he wasn't looking for just anything, his son wanted him. It astonished him and shook him to the core.

He put his arm around Jack and led him to a bench. There had been thirty years of chill between them, each of their making.

The drizzle was turning to a driving rain. As they hit

the bench, so Jack slumped, sobbing, into his father's arms. Laying his head into his lap. Michael gripped him tightly as his exhausted sobs increased. His son was shaking with desperation. Michael held him as if he were a small boy, and he began to weep as well. They rocked, in silence, holding each other. For the first time in their lives.

Amy had taken Sarah to St James's Park, where she'd arranged to meet Susan. She was sheltering from the rain in the tea room when Alain walked in. He came up to her table. Amy looked around for Susan.

'What are you doing here? Where's Susan?'

He stood awkwardly for a moment.

'She couldn't come. She's had to go to the doctor.'

There was a look of deep seriousness on his face.

'What's wrong? What is it?' Amy asked, desperately.

He didn't seem to know whether to sit or stand.

'She um . . . she . . . she thinks she's pregnant,' he said.

Amy looked down at the table.

'I see.' She took a sip of her coffee. 'Congratulations.'

'Thanks,' he said.

'You must be very happy.'

Silence.

'Amy . . .?' Alain floundered. She snatched Sarah up and began pulling down the shade on the pram.

'We've got to go . . .' she said. She walked out, leaving him standing there.

When Jack got home, Amy was in the kitchen, slowly turning a teaspoon around in a coffee cup. He felt exhausted.

'Hi,' he said. 'Is she asleep?'

'Yes,' said Amy, 'she was very tired.' He looked at her. Her eyes were red and she had obviously been crying. It was awful to see her like this. He took a deep breath and tried to make himself feel stronger for her.

'Amy, what's the matter? What's happened?'

'Nothing,' she said, and looked away from him.

'You've been crying. What is it? Has my mother been round?'

Amy looked back at him and laughed weakly. 'No . . .'

'You've seen the phone bill?'

Jack had never known anyone who needed to call their mother quite so much as Amy.

'Don't worry about it. It's only money – my money admittedly, but only money . . .' It wasn't having the desired effect. 'What's wrong?' he said, suddenly beginning to realise. 'Alain?'

She closed her mouth firmly and began to nod.

'Want to talk about it?'

Then she shook her head and burst into tears. My God, what a day of tears, thought Jack. He braced himself. No matter how he felt himself, he couldn't bear to see her like this.

'Come on, sit down,' he said, putting his arm around her and leading her to the sofa. She flopped down and Jack went to put the kettle on. She tried to smile, it was such an English thing for him to do. But she could see the genuine sympathy in his eyes.

Jack did feel for her. She'd always appeared so resilient but now she seemed as stranded here in London as he was. He hadn't realised how serious the relationship between Alain and her had been. They talked it through.

Later in the evening the telephone rang for Amy. Jack let her take it alone and went upstairs until he heard the receiver replaced.

'That was Susan,' said Amy, a range of bemused expressions glancing across her face.

'Yes?' said Jack.

'She's not pregnant. She was wrong.' She wiped her nose on her sleeve. 'It was a false alarm. Oh God, this is so stupid.'

Jack smiled, and smoothed the back of her hand, then he gripped it in encouragement.

'D'you still love him?' he asked.

She shook her head. 'I don't know. I don't think so . . . oh, I don't know.'

Jack thought about Alain. He'd found him entirely disagreeable in every way. But there's no accounting for taste.

'Oh dear,' he said, 'you are in a pickle.'

She smiled, 'pickle' was such an English way, again, to describe the complete mess she'd got herself into in this country. But it cheered her up, it was a comforting, homely expression for him to use. Sometimes, she realised, that when the British understate, maybe, just maybe, it's because they mean it the most. He was a good man, and looked today as if he'd been crying himself.

'Jack,' she said, 'I think I may have to go home.'

She saw the sudden pain in his eyes, as he squeezed her hand, and the tears began to fall from her eyes again.

'All right, all right,' he said softly. 'Let's talk about this again tomorrow.'

It was time for bed. The day had been far too emotional for both of them. They walked together up the stairs and went to their rooms. Both of them needed a good solid rest. Tomorrow was another day.

23

There was frost on the ground again and the trees of the square had a stark sparkle to them.

The lilac in the garden didn't look as if it was going to survive the winter after its severe pruning, both after his mother's direction and later, after the onslaught of William's secateurs. Jack didn't mind at all, he'd always found it a morbid sort of tree. The blooms just hung there swaying with a funereal purple, limp and hang-dog like groups of mourners. But the crocuses and the narcissi that Amy had planted before Christmas were jumping up through the hard ground.

This year, Jack decided, he'd grow roses, and he'd plant honeysuckle and fill the small garden through the French windows with great colourful, scented blooms. And they'd have daft little garden parties in the summer, with bunting and taramasalata, and big jugs of Pimm's.

Maybe he'd make a sandpit in the garden for Sarah. But then he remembered the sandpit that he had as a boy, in the select perfect garden in Camberley. All the local cats used to shit in it.

Sarah would soon be a year old. It was the day for Sarah's booster jab. Jack was at work and Margaret came round to drive Amy and Sarah to the clinic. Margaret had little to say to Amy in the car. Amy would have much preferred to have taken a taxi, but Margaret didn't seem to think her capable of anything so technical as a measles jab. If Jack knew, he'd be furious, thought Amy.

They sat in the waiting-room, Amy nervously flicking through a pile of ancient magazines, and Margaret looking down her nose at the other patients. A child, about the same age as Sarah, was crying miserably and she glared at its mother. The young woman was chewing gum and there was a whiff of dry cleaning fluid about her. Margaret disliked mixing with the public in waiting-rooms like this. She hoped that the American girl appreciated the sacrifice she had made. Another woman came in with a baby who looked much nicer, albeit severely flustered by the whole affair. Margaret recognised her from the organic cheese shop in the high street.

A young doctor poked his head around the surgery door.

'Sarah Guscott?' he said.

'That's us!' said Margaret, poking Amy forcefully in the ribs. The girl was in a dream. Amy was cross, she just wasn't used to the baby being addressed by her full name, that was all. She was too small to answer to a surname. It didn't seem unreasonable to Amy.

They went into the surgery.

'Right, just slip her shorts off,' said the doctor. Sarah was gurgling happily about the whole performance.

'She'll feel a little jab, nothing more,' said the doctor as he pierced the little bottle with the syringe. Amy began to look a bit green around the gills.

'Are you all right?' said the doctor.

Margaret moved in. 'I think you'd better pass my granddaughter to me,' she said, shaking her head. 'We don't want her dropped to the floor, do we, doctor?'

Amy looked at the wall as the needle went in. There

was a little whimper from Sarah. Amy gripped on to her chair.

Sarah gave out a pitiful little cry. Amy lost focus, began to sway and fell to the floor in a dead faint.

Margaret drove Amy back in silence. The girl was as pale as porcelain. Just not tough enough for the job. Finally Margaret spoke her mind.

'You're not exactly what you might call a natural at this, are you?'

Amy stared miserably out of the window, and then down at Sarah for reassurance.

'Admittedly he seems to want you around, and that's fine,' continued Margaret. 'But don't get a false impression of your situation. He's very vulnerable at the moment.'

Blood rushed suddenly back to Amy's face now.

'What are you saying?' she asked.

Margaret drove in silence for a moment as they turned into the square.

'I think you know what I'm saying, dear,' she said.

They pulled up and Amy got Sarah out of the car as quickly as she could.

'I'm glad we had our little chat,' said Margaret. 'I won't come in. Goodbye, Sarah,' she said, and drove off.

Amy watched her go, seething for a moment. She was so horribly English it made Amy want to go straight to the gun store. She climbed the steps to the house.

As she put her key in the deadlock she found that the door was already open. She entered the house cautiously. The front door was never left recklessly open like this.

'Didn't we lock this when we went out?' said Amy to

Sarah. She could hear singing from the basement and there was an overpowering smell of alcohol on the stairs wafting up in great sweet acidic waves.

'Hello?' called Amy.

She knew the song from old movies but couldn't place it. It was the Eton Boating Song, and it was William's voice that was slurring it out.

The basement floor, in which all the living took place in this house, was filled with dust. It had been transformed from a comfortable room with a fine maple floor, a newly organised kitchen and sofas to relax on, into something that looked like a flat in West Beirut. It was mayhem, and in the middle of it all, William was pissed out of his brains, gripping on to a worktop, smiling at her while he poured the remains of several liqueur bottles into a pint pot. He made himself up a fearsome mixture of Benedictine, tequila and cherry brandy. He raised it to his lips and drew deep.

Amy looked around again. The pictures were at angles on the walls. The beautiful floor was awash with ash and drink. There were tea-towels everywhere, abandoned beside bottles of detergent. Everything was out of the cupboards and scattered around in toppled heaps. The contents of the laundry basket and the washing machine were strewn across the room. The fridge door was open and everything that had been in it was laid in random piles around the kitchen. The ice compartment was dripping and a puddle stretched across the floor.

It looked as if there'd been a flood that had brought mud down with it from the mountains. The spice drawer was open, with all its contents spilled, and there were the muddy prints around the walls where William had struggled to retain his balance.

Amy could barely breathe and Sarah was choking on the air of grime and spice dust.

'Bill!' screamed Amy.

Swaying considerably he pulled himself up and looked at her sternly.

'My name,' he said, 'is William. I am not something you call for at the end of a meal.'

She wasn't listening to him. She looked around at the devastation of the room again.

'What are you doing?!' she screamed. 'What the hell do you think you're doing?'

His head wavered for a moment, and he took an olympic gulp from the pint pot of mixed liqueur dregs.

'Spring cleaning!' he said, triumphantly.

She shook her head. She didn't know what to do with Sarah, she couldn't possibly put her down here. She cleared a space on the sofa.

'Look at the state of this place,' she said.

William smiled happily. 'It always looks worse before it looks better,' he said. The destruction that he had caused obviously seemed reasonable to him.

'If Jack sees you like this you'll lose your job,' Amy reminded him.

William gripped on to the worktop and pulled himself up again, swinging his pint pot with bravado. 'Deservedly so,' he said. 'I wouldn't employ me. Would you? Mind you, I wouldn't employ you! Strange fellow, this Jack.' She shook her head, he was full of such shit. It brought back memories of her father, and his drunken, overpowering breath. The smell that undermined every word he said to her. The total self-obsession.

William was struggling to stay upright, with a silly grin on his face. Then, all of a sudden, his eyes began to flutter and he collapsed. He went swiftly down and there was an awful crack as his head hit the floor. Then silence.

The doorbell was ringing upstairs.

Amy looked between the empty space behind the worktop and the stairs to the door.

'I say,' said William's voice. 'You wouldn't be a doll and answer that, would you?'

Amy went to the door. It was Phil. When she led her down the stairs all Phil could say was, 'My God . . . Jack'll kill him.'

William was as happy being lateral as he had been vertical. He lay where he was and merrily hummed the Eton Boating Song while Amy and Phil mounted the gargantuan task of restoring the kitchen. Baby Sarah was picking stray raisins from the jars he'd busted off William's face. He was having a delightful time while the two women worked. They scrubbed the place with an urgent fury. Jack was expected home at any minute. They could have used an industrial vacuum to begin with. Even the window panes were covered with a thick film of crap, like the leaded lights to the windows in the snug of a City pub. It seemed to take for ever, and when it was done they were exhausted and their hands red raw.

Both Amy and Phil looked up at the same time, as they heard the familiar sound of Jack's car pulling up outside.

'He's back,' said Amy.

William's hands gripped the worktop and he pulled himself up on receipt of the news. 'He's, back . . . maaaaaarvelous!'

Phil and Amy looked at each other very seriously.

'We've got to get him out of here,' said Phil.

'Take him out by the basement steps as soon as Jack comes through the front door,' said Amy. William smiled at her. Maybe she wasn't such a bad girl after all, she'd been a great help with the spring cleaning.

Phil struggled to keep William upright, and as Jack came down the steps, so she pushed him through the basement door and up into the street. But as soon as they were on the pavement he managed to free himself and began walking back up the front steps to re-enter the house by the front door. Phil grabbed him by the shoulders and pulled him back down the steps and towards her car. She leaned him against it as she reached for her keys. His head flopped on to the roof of the car.

'Would you like me to drive?' he said.

Phil looked at this absolutely most ridiculous of men and laughed out loud. 'I think not,' she said.

'Probably wise,' said William, nodding. She pushed his head in through the door and belted him in. She turned her key in the ignition.

'Where do you live, William?'

He turned towards her slowly. 'On the very edge, madam . . . the very edge,' he said. And then he passed out, his head slowly sliding into her lap, where he instantly began to snore, contentedly, like a small boy.

'Oh God . . .' said Phil.

Jack stood in the kitchen looking at Amy. She looked a bit frazzled this evening. 'What's wrong?' he asked. She shook her head. Jack looked around the room, everything was spotless. There was the fresh smell of pine.

He smiled. 'Has William been back?' he said.

'Very much so,' said Amy.

Jack went over to pick Sarah up. She had a quizzical expression too. 'What's the matter, darling? Aren't you pleased to see Daddy?' He turned to Amy. 'How was her jab?'

'Fine. She cried a bit, that's all.'

'I'm sure I wouldn't be nearly so brave, and that's just watching.'

'Oh, it's not so big a deal for them,' said Amy.

'Poor little thing,' he said, kissing her.

24

Jack rolled his head on the pillow and looked at Amy as she stared at him. He groaned deeply. She shook her head, and held out a mug of hot lemon. He waved his hand weakly in the direction of the bedside locker. He was far too ill to take it right now.

'Who was that who came round?' he asked, quietly.

'Your mother.'

'Why didn't she come up?' he asked.

'She was in a rush.'

Jack looked hurt. 'What did she come for?'

'She came to see if there was anything she could do. I told her she could either take Sarah off my hands or she could look after you. So she took Sarah.'

'Oh,' he said sadly. 'Did she ask how I was?'

'Um, no, she didn't actually. She was just pleased that Sarah had got over her cold so much better than you. How are you feeling?'

'Terrible,' he said, staring up at the ceiling. 'Morale is low and the will to live is weak. I'll be surprised if I pull through.'

Amy looked out into the square before she cracked up. Men were just the most pathetic things in the world when they caught a cold. The reason they couldn't discover a cure for it was probably because there's simply no cure for men.

'I just hope I'll be well enough for Sarah's birthday party,' he said.

'You will be.'

'But what if it's not a cold?' he asked. 'What if it's Hong Kong 'flu. Or Brazilian bronchitis . . . or something . . .'

She picked up a copy of *The Home Doctor* which was lying on his duvet. Its pages were heavily thumbed. Its spine was broken in several places.

'I think you've been taking this too seriously,' she said.

'I'm confined to bed, I've got to have something to read,' he said, with a terrible sense of injustice playing across his face. 'It's as much as I can do to turn the pages.'

'It's probably just a vitamin B deficiency,' she said, 'that comes from living in England. No sunshine.'

He looked at her seriously. 'D'you think? Perhaps it's this new thing SAD – seasonal deficiency something-or-other?'

'Well it's certainly sad,' she said. 'Now is there anything else I can do?'

'No. There's probably nothing anyone can do.'

'Are you sure?'

He looked up at her again, pouting weakly. 'Would you mind awfully giving me a cuddle?' he said. She raised her eyebrows and sat on the edge of his bed. He laid his head in her lap while she stroked his hair.

'I thought I was supposed to be Sarah's nanny,' she said.

'It was never specific in the job description.'

'This job,' said Amy, 'could never be described.'

Jack didn't die, in fact he was better the next morning and went out to buy a camcorder. His excuse for the extravagance was that you only have a first birthday once, and you can't be expected to remember it yourself. It was his duty as a father to record it for her, she'd never forgive him if he didn't. He was quite delighted with the new toy and leapt around the house with it making 'movies'. The phone rang. 'If it's the office,' he said, 'tell them I'm very, very ill. Probably won't survive.' He swirled around her videotaping her as she made his excuses.

On the day of Sarah's birthday everyone came to tea. Phil, Margaret and Michael, that is, and William, of course, who'd returned from the square and resumed his former duties.

After the party was over Jack sat down to watch the video he'd made of it while Amy cleared away the things in the kitchen. Sarah was playing on the carpet with her new toys.

The opening shots were a bit shaky, but the screen settled down as it focused on the single candle burning on the cake. As the camera moved the candle burned a waving trail across the screen. Then Sarah appeared, her eyes bright and shining, reflecting the candle's flame. The camera pulled back to show the little party singing 'Happy Birthday'. William's voice booming out as if he were leading a hymn in chapel. Michael mouthing silently. Margaret with a fixed look on her face as if she were auditioning for the local light operatic. Phil holding little Sarah's hand. Amy waving her napkin.

Jack grinned broadly. What an extraordinary collection of people his household contained.

Sarah was excited. She knew all this attention was for her, and was thrilled by it. She'd never been so close to a flame before. Even the adults were getting on for once.

The candle was blown out and the shot changed to a mayhem of wrapping paper across the floor, with Sarah in the middle of it. She was equally pleased with the wrapping paper as she was with the presents. Then William turned to face the camera, like someone in an old cine film not quite sure how to pose for a moving picture. Then another shot of William came up in which he was looking eminently more relaxed, sitting happily on the sofa with Phil, enjoying a cup of tea with her. He raised his tea cup and said, 'Cheers'. They giggled like children.

The camera panned to see Amy playing with Sarah, squatting on the carpet. Amy really did look at home, in the middle of it all. The two were so natural together.

Then the real baby pulled herself up in front of the screen, recognising herself and Amy. She turned to Jack, laughing. He blew her a kiss and she toddled over from the screen to sit in his lap and watch the pictures of her party. He cuddled her. As he watched Sarah on the screen being held by Amy, he looked away from the screen to the mantelpiece where there was a framed photograph of Sarah. There was a sudden terrible lump in his throat. His wife had been denied the joy of holding her child. Sarah's birthday would also for ever be the anniversary of her mother's death.

It was quite late when Jack finally put Sarah to bed. The door opened and Amy came in, dressed for bed in her T-shirt. This room was always gently soothing, with the glow of the night light from inside a painted ceramic toadstool, and the abundance of soft, furry animals sitting around the room and on the window ledges.

'She stayed up late,' said Amy.

'She's a party girl,'

Amy sat down on the floor and leaned her head against the wall.

'Weird day for you,' she said.

He sighed briefly.

'It was fine.' He nodded his head a little. He'd come through it much better than he'd thought possible. He'd not 'made a fool of himself', as his mother would say.

Amy looked into Sarah's bed.

'What'll you tell her about Sarah?'

'Everything I suppose,' he said. 'I tell her stuff now. I know she doesn't understand but I'm terrified I'll forget if I don't. I don't mean forget her, but things, little things. So I tell her to remind me. Maybe I should write it down.' He paused for a moment, they'd never really spoken like this.

'I've kept her perfume and hairspray for her to smell when she's older. Because that's how I remember Sarah in the morning. Silly, really,' he said.

'No, I don't think so,' said Amy. 'You can't smell a photograph.'

She looked at him. He was a good man, and she admired him.

'What does it feel like losing your wife?' she asked. 'I mean, my dad, I know what my mother felt, but he was sixty-five. She was?'

'Twenty-nine. Twenty-nine years old. 24th February 1965.'

'So young.'

'Yes.'

He sunk down to the floor, and leaned against the wall.

'You know when there's something really important you should've done and you haven't? Your stomach turns when you remember? It's like that every morning when you wake up. You feel sick. Because for a second when you open your eyes everything's fine. Then it hits you. You remember. And simple things terrify you: the book she was reading still open where she left it by the bed. Her writing on cheque-book stubs. Her lipstick on a wine glass. Because what's touched them is dead and it's impossible to believe.'

Tears were beginning to course down his cheeks.

'But it's true. She's gone. Gone for good, and that's that,' he said.

They sat in silence.

Amy slowly got up.

'I think you're very brave,' she said.

The baby was sleeping soundly and the square was absolutely quiet tonight.

'I think I must go to bed,' he said. He stood up and Amy walked towards him.

'I know this is against the rules, but come here,' she said. She put her arms around him and hugged him. She kissed him gently on the lips.

'Good night,' she said.

'Good night.'

He looked down at the little bed.

'Good night Sarah,' he whispered. Amy saw a flash across his face as it suddenly grew sad. It hadn't really occurred to her until this moment that every time he said 'Good night Sarah' he was also saying 'Goodbye' to his wife. As she looked at him, staring lovingly at his baby, she felt a strange flutter inside.

25

Amy's friend, Susan, was still in London and she'd invited Amy round to dinner. It had worked out fine, Jack was having a working dinner at home.

Amy took with her the packs of photographs she'd taken at Sarah's birthday party. They sat looking at them, the table bearing the remains of an extravagant bolognaise. They'd had a good, fun evening, just like the old times.

'I didn't think it would suit you this well,' said Susan.

'What?'

'Motherhood.'

'Oh, sure, motherhood!' said Amy, almost swiping her with the photos. She began putting them back in their envelope. Susan was building up to something, Amy could see it on her face. She fiddled with the photographs for a moment.

'Have you fallen in love with him?' asked Susan.

'What? Of course not' said Amy, dropping one of the photographs to the floor. 'I just feel sorry for him.' She picked up the photograph, little Sarah, beaming with her arms around her neck. She turned it towards Susan.

'Mind you, she doesn't help. She could make you think you were in love with anyone.'

Amy pulled herself up quickly. What had she just said? She'd practically confirmed Susan's question.

'Talking of love . . .' she said swiftly, 'how are things with Alain? You've not mentioned him all evening.'

'Oh things are terrific,' Susan replied. 'I haven't seen him for months, not since I kicked him out after we found out I wasn't pregnant. He practically threw a party.' Strange question for Amy to ask, thought Susan. She was obviously trying to avoid the real subject of Jack.

Nevertheless they finished their evening with a thoroughly comprehensive bitching session on the subject of Alain.

But as Amy went home, she thought about what Susan had said about Jack.

Amy got back to the square and let herself in. The lights were on in the downstairs room and she could hear voices. She could also hear very distraught screaming from the nursery, which was being ignored. She dashed up the stairs. Sarah was in a sweat and a tangle, all tied up in the bedclothes.

Downstairs Jack and Anna had finished dinner. Ella Fitzgerald was playing on the CD and Jack poured Anna another glass of dessert wine.

Anna was resting her head on her elbow, relaxed, and looking at Jack across the dining table. They were both very mellow and had enjoyed a fine evening. Anna was looking particularly sultry tonight, and Jack was feeling warm, warm with drink and warm with her company. They had seen a great deal of each other over the last months.

Anna sipped from her glass.

'I thought we could go out on Saturday afternoon,' she said. 'Up to Marlow. Go on the river. Have a picnic.'

'Mmm . . .' murmured Jack, 'that'd be nice.' He

looked so handsome when wine and low lighting enlarged his pupils and he was finally, and ultimately, approachable. Relaxed, charming . . . warm.

They both sighed with the pleasure of the evening, and the thought of the river.

'Very nice,' said Jack. 'Sarah's never been in a boat before.'

Anna looked down at her glass. 'I was thinking more of just the two of us. We could stay over.'

'Ah . . .' said Jack.

'Couldn't your mother look after Sarah? We could pick her up on Sunday.'

'No.'

'What about Phil?'

Jack heaved a sigh and reached for the wine bottle.

'No. The weekend's the only time I really get with her. I wouldn't enjoy it.'

She took the wine bottle from him and swirled it in front of his face before pouring a measure into her glass.

'I think you would . . .' she said. She leaned over the table towards him. They began to kiss. Their mouths were sweet with the muscat wine.

Amy burst into the room, clutching a screaming Sarah.

Jack leapt up, and Anna reached to fasten the top button of her blouse.

'Please don't let me interrupt,' said Amy. 'I didn't realise you were still eating.'

'What's the matter?' said Jack. 'When did you come in?'

Amy didn't answer but walked over to the baby alarm sitting on the dresser. She flicked the button and the red light came on.

'You need to switch these on both ends, you know,' she said, glaring at Anna, suspecting that it was her who'd switched it off.

Jack turned the CD down, guiltily.

'What's wrong with her?'

'Didn't you hear her?' asked Amy. 'She's been screaming for I don't know how long.' She looked between him and Anna again. 'I guess it's difficult with Ella Fitzgerald in one ear and her in the other.'

She picked up Sarah's bottle and swept out of the room, back to the nursery.

Jack looked at Anna. He didn't know what to say.

'Excuse me a moment,' he said.

Jack walked into the nursery, where Amy was feeding the baby.

He stood and stared at her. 'With respect,' he said, 'I don't think you should talk to me like that. You're forgetting she is my child.'

Amy rounded on him.

'Then – with respect – act like her father!'

She hated that awful English expression, with respect, it always meant with none at all. It was the phrase they used when all respect was gone.

'What have I done that's so wrong?' he said, defending himself. 'All I did was to forget to turn the thing on.'

'You were in charge of the baby.'

'And I was here in the house!' he said furiously.

Amy narrowed her eyes and nodded. 'Trying to get laid,' she said.

'So?'

There was a pause. He was trying to get laid!

'What kind of mother d'you suppose she'd make?'

He hadn't supposed anything of the sort.

'Who, Anna? What's that got to do with anything?'

'Work it out for yourself,' said Amy. For a decent man he could be so absolutely blind.

'What is this?' he said. 'Going to bed with someone is going to bed with them, Amy, not a "will you come and spend the rest of your life with me?". I wouldn't dream of living with Anna any more than she would with me. I'd never live it down at work for a start and I'd certainly never trust her with Sarah. It's not serious, it's just a bit of fun. She knows that.'

He'd finished his speech and was rather pleased with it. Amy just stood there with a smirk on her face. She looked towards the baby alarm and its little red light.

'Well if she didn't before, she certainly does now,' she said.

Oh, my God, thought Jack, and dashed down the stairs.

Anna's glass, still half full, was abandoned on the table. He looked around him. She had gone.

His mind raced through what he'd just said. He stared at the baby alarm on the dresser. Just a bit of fun . . . wouldn't dream of living with her . . . never trust her with Sarah . . . never live it down at work.

He was furious with himself. Why had he said those things? Who was he trying to please this time? Amy?

He was furious with her.

He walked back into the nursery.

'Are you happy now?' he said. She must have known what she had done. It was almost as if she'd planned it, he thought.

'I don't give a shit, to be honest,' she said.

'Oh no?'

She withered and shook her head, turning away from him.

'I want to put the baby down. Please go away.'

He was incensed.

'Give her to me.'

'No,' she said. 'You've been drinking, you'll upset her.'

Jack thought for a moment. How dare she lecture him like this in his own house? And added to this she seemed to be suddenly under the illusion that Sarah was her own baby. He was hardly drunk. The offence of her accusation stuck in his craw. His anger with her was growing. She stood over the baby as if she suddenly imagined herself to be some sort of saintly figure; a Florence Nightingale of the nursery.

'I know what this is all about,' he said. 'You're jealous. My mother was right!'

'What!?'

'You're angry because you're jealous. All that crap about the Frenchman and going home. You never went because you've got it too good here.'

She could not believe he was saying this.

'Too good here? You are unbelievable,' she said. 'Truly incredible.'

What a typical Californian expression, he thought.

Jack stood and waited for a few minutes. He knew how to let the moment of tension die down in a courtroom.

Finally he looked at her, gathering himself together.

'So you're not angry?'

'Oh, I'm angry,' she said. 'Oh yes, I'm angry all right.'

'With me?'

'Absolutely with you!' she spat. There was a fire in her eyes.

He looked at her hard for a while. She had become absolutely unreasonable now. She'd lost her grip of the whole situation, he thought. He was victorious.

'I knew it. Why?' he said.

Amy braced herself.

'Because you go around like a single man without a care in the world. You never come home, you're always in the pub or at a party, or out at dinner. You always put yourself first. You haven't been back in time to put her to bed for a week. Do you know that?'

'God, this is just like being married,' said Jack, weary with arguing.

'It may be for you but it sure as hell isn't for me.'

Jack began to lose the cool that he'd just struggled to regain.

'Well, if you don't like it . . .'

They stared at each other. Very slowly the angry fire that was in Amy's eyes changed to a cold look of resignation.

'Fine,' said Amy and settled Sarah in her cot. 'You don't deserve her. You're too selfish to be a father.'

She walked out and headed for her own room. Jack followed her, walking drunkenly, as he remembered the words Sarah had said to him the night before she died. He replayed the evening again in his mind: Pamela saying, 'You'll make a fabulous father, Jack' and Sarah's reply, 'He won't. He's too selfish.'

He shook his head for a moment, but it did no good. He looked up at Amy. She was throwing things into a suitcase and pulling T-shirts down from the window frame.

'What're you doing?' Asked Jack.

'What does it look like I'm doing?'

He looked at her bags. They looked just as they did when she arrived. She seemed to really mean it.

'Oh great, we have an argument and you go. Terrific.

That's fantastic. Is this going to happen every time we have a row?'

She clicked her suitcase shut.

'And what exactly am I supposed to do now?'

She slid the suitcase from the bed.

'You'll be OK,' she said. 'You'll get yourself a nice English nanny, till Sarah's old enough to go to school and then you'll send her away – "it's what she wanted" – and then when she doesn't turn out the way you want you can blame everyone else. Why not? It's your right. Isn't that the English way?'

'Do you have any idea what I am going through?' he said. 'Do you have any conception of how hard it is for me just to get through every day? Do you? D'you ever think about that? At all?'

'Yes. I do. Constantly,' she said, calmly.

'Then why can't you make allowances? God alone knows I've made enough for you.' Jack watched her as she pulled up her things. He stood his ground. 'Well fine, go! And you're right, I will get myself a nanny. Someone who knows her job and her place!'

Amy smiled.

'I'm sure you will. I'll pick up the rest of my stuff next week.'

'Just make sure I'm at work,' Jack threw back. Amy walked out of the room, leaving him staring at the wall as he listened to her steps descending the stairs.

He walked slowly downstairs. There were the remains of a dinner party on the table, there was lipstick on a glass.

26

As telephone calls go, this was one of the toughest he'd ever made. It was eight o'clock in the morning and both he and Sarah had slept badly. Now he was simply going to have to ask his mother for help. He felt there was no way that he could just take the day off work to look after her. Not today.

'Well it's really very awkward, darling,' said his mother. 'You have put me on the spot a little . . .'

Jack was convinced she was enjoying every minute of it. The woman who was round here at the drop of a hat, on any implausible mission, was now playing hard to get.

'You mean the American girl has just left you entirely in the lurch?'

She wanted to wring it out of him.

'Well no, we had, er . . . she had mentioned she might have to go back to the States . . . some time ago.' He wasn't so much making excuses for her as for his own stupidity in hiring her in the first place.

'And now she's just upped and gone, and left you holding the baby, as it were. Well, quite exactly that, darling,' Margaret said with glee. 'Who'd have thought it? Well, of course, as you know I always felt . . .'

'Mum, look, I'm really sorry to have to ask you but I can't possibly take the day off, I've got a very big meeting first thing,' Jack said. And it was a big meeting. It was going to be hell facing Anna but it had to be taken on the chin right away. If he didn't go to work she'd presume he was running.

'Well then,' said Margaret, with a low, enduring sigh, 'I suppose I shall have to step into the breach once more.'

'Good, good,' said Jack, relieved, 'can you come straight over?'

'Mmm . . .' she said, drawing out the agony a little longer, but at the same time entirely thrilled that he'd called on her for help. 'It'll mean getting the Volvo out. Your father's gone hairing off in my little Astra.'

'Right, excellent, I'll see you in a little while.'

Margaret arrived and took over Sarah. Allowing Jack to drive off to face a truly dreadful day at West, West & Purnell.

As he walked towards Anna's office door she appeared to be absorbed in a sheath of papers, scribbling frantically on little yellow Post-it notes. He stopped in her doorway. Perhaps it would be best to leave it, take her for a drink after work. No, she'd never do that. She'd probably quite reasonably suggest that there was nothing really to discuss; it had all been covered on that fateful intercom. He was fixed to the spot by his dilemma.

Anna looked up and smiled.

'Good morning, Jack,' she said politely. The smile on her face was courteous, business-like.

Oh God, thought Jack, I'd sooner she threw something at me. Screamed, showed some anger. But, of course, she never would.

'I'm . . .' Jack began flapping his hands. 'I'm . . . so sorry,' he said.

She scribbled on another Post-it and looked back up at him.

'Really, Jack,' she said, 'there's no need to come in here with your tail between your legs. We're both experienced adults. Reasonable people. It really doesn't matter at all.'

'It's just, I . . .'

'There's no need to say anything. We tried, but fortunately we have learnt in time not to be foolish with each other.'

She was being so reasonable he felt even worse. He cursed himself for making a mess of things. A mess of everything.

'Well, I . . .' he floundered again, 'I guess I'll put my mother off for Sunday lunch.'

'Probably best,' said Anna. Now she had the look on her face which she used at the end of partners' meetings. The signal that business had been concluded. Everything was satisfactorily settled.

Jack attempted a smile before walking to his office. He glanced down at her desk. This morning she had bought herself a large bouquet of flowers. The greater part of which was made up of roses.

Over the course of this week Jack took to taking long walks in his lunch hour. He wouldn't really admit to himself what it was he was looking for in the faces of the crowds on the London streets. He often found himself wandering in the direction of Susan's warehouse, or the French brasserie.

On Wednesday evening he was held up in traffic on the way home from the office. He began to panic, he really didn't want to be late home. The new nanny had only been there for three days. He tore into the house. There in the hallway was Miss Cartwright, putting her coat on over her blue guernsey and pearls. She was looking at her watch.

'I'm late, I'm sorry,' he said breathlessly.

She flashed a short efficient smile, like a schoolmistress reproving a miscreant of five years old.

'Three minutes,' she said. 'Don't worry. I'm sure it won't happen again.'

'Where's Sarah?' he asked, recovering himself.

'Baby's bathed and bedded.'

God, it irritated him that she still couldn't use Sarah's name.

'But I wanted to give her her bath,' he protested. 'It's only six-thirty, for God's sake.'

'Then count your blessings,' she said, pertly. Her coat was on and she picked up her little document case. What on earth a nanny required a document case for defeated Jack.

'Well, what am I supposed to do now?' he said.

'I don't know. I'm your nanny, not your social secretary,' she said.

Her hand was on the latch. White bony knuckles itching to escape the house and the sleeping baby upstairs.

'Um, could you babysit next Thursday?' he asked.

She slid her hand into her thin little leather document case and pulled out her Filofax.

'Let me see . . . thought so . . . bridge, sorry.'

She closed the door behind her, leaving Jack forlorn in the hallway. Bridge was the bane of his domestic life.

Jack wandered sadly up to the nursery where Sarah was lying wide awake, but staring dolefully as if she'd had a most difficult day too. She looked bored and miserable. It was appalling to see in such a little girl. He held her until she fell asleep.

He went into Amy's room. It was starkly, and suddenly bare. She had obviously been here today to collect her things. Only the papier mâché mirror, with the starfish and the sea horses that he'd bought for her that day at Camden Market remained on the wall. It was at an angle and he straightened it. She'd obviously gone to take it and then changed her mind. The fact that it had been so calculatedly left behind made it worse. He reached to take it down and caught sight of himself in it. He looked as bored and sad as little Sarah.

Now he was stuck with Miss Starch Knickers. It was the only solution, of course, and he'd been too weak to fight his mother when she'd seen her moment at last and telephoned her friend Felicity.

He went down to the kitchen and opened a can of condensed soup. The sad man's dinner, he'd always called it. He switched on the television. A programme about the day's proceedings in the House of Lords.

There seemed to be a national conspiracy to bore him to death.

He looked around the kitchen. The draining board was absolutely spotless. There were no grains of coffee spilled. No rings of milk on the worktops. No burnt bread crumbs around the toaster, or wayward sachets of burger relish strewn across the table. No bras or panties spilling from the laundry basket. No CDs left out of their cases. Whatever Miss Cartwright did in this house during the day was left to pure conjecture. There was no stamp of any human presence whatsoever.

Mid-evening the doorbell rang and broke into his boredom. He leapt up and ran to the door. It was William. He was dressed in a new tweed jacket and cavalry twill trousers. He looked terribly sober, in every respect.

'William! Come in!' said Jack.

William regarded him for a moment, looking him up and down. The boy looked as if he'd dined off a dinner of condensed soup and whisky.

'I won't, thank you,' he said firmly.

'OK, so what can I do for you?'

'I just came to say I think you're a fool. An unconscionably stupid, blinkered idiot.'

He was serious.

'Well, thank you,' said Jack.

'My pleasure.' William turned on the soles of his new shoes and began walking back into the square. Jack couldn't really believe that this was it, that he'd rung at his door expressly to say this.

Jack called after him.

'You couldn't babysit Thursday, could you?'

William walked on without turning.

'Certainly not.'

Jack stood on his top step watching William walk away and turn out of the square. The blossom on the ornamental cherry trees was late this year. There was a chill in the air.

The following weekend was a desolate affair. It was a relief to have no Miss Cartwright about the house, but there was nothing else about the house either. Sarah had an odd look on her face as if she blamed him for the sudden absence of her friend Amy. And she would, of course, have been right.

He pushed her along Islington High Street, aimlessly

227

gazing at the shop fronts. Sometimes stopping to look in the windows of shops in which he had no interest whatsoever. Then Sarah would begin to sniff.

He'd not seen William since Wednesday. He was keeping his distance, Jack presumed, since the arrival of the fearsome Miss Cartwright. She seemed to have drained every spark of life from the house. Why didn't she leave magazines on the floor, flick through his books and leave them in disarray? She didn't even appear to drink his coffee while he was at work. He imagined she must bring a thermos flask with her, and sandwiches, or salmon pinwheels, in a tupperware box for her lunch. He wondered what she did for sex. He winced. He pulled himself up short, he was staring into a shop window full of lingerie and the assistants were looking back at him. It hadn't even registered.

He got into a cab and went to Camden Lock Market. He was, perhaps, still looking for a face in the crowd. Perhaps she would be feeling like him and would return to that bench they'd sat on, eating pizza, holding court. But no, there was no face in the crowd.

Sarah looked up at him accusingly. He tickled her under the chin but she didn't give out that little giggle that thrilled him so much.

He got in a cab to Alain's brasserie.

He walked in slightly nervously, looking all about him. It looked a lot dirtier than it had when he'd first come here. There were scuff marks on the wooden floor. There were tourists in day-glo anoraks, hardened against the chill London weather.

There was a new waitress. She was dark, and Spanish-looking, with heavy eyebrows, and she served the customers sullenly, as if it were beneath her. Jack sat

Sarah on the bar and ordered a beer from Alain. Alain had a quizzical, amused expression on his face as he passed the beer over. Jack was conscious of the fact that Alain felt that he had won.

Sarah sat pulling grapes out of a bowl of fruit on the bar top while they talked.

'I wouldn't mind seeing her myself. When did she leave?' asked Alain.

'Almost four weeks ago' said Jack. It irritated him to have to come here and give himself up to this man.

'She's probably back in the States. Have you tried her mother?'

'No,' said Jack. 'Have you got her number?'

'Sorry,' said Alain, with a little quiver of pleasure playing below his lips. Jack stared at the wooden floor. Watched as the sullen waitress passed. Looked back at the self-satisfied Alain.

'Well if you do see her,' he said.

'I'll tell her to call,' said Alain, magnanimously.

Jack pulled Sarah away from the fruit bowl, and walked slowly out of the brasserie. Alain watched him go.

Alain was glad to see Jack so low. He clicked his fingers at the sullen Spanish waitress and called her attention to the corner table, who needed more beers. Then he walked into the kitchen. He enjoyed the atmosphere of the kitchen. The steam, the smell of burning oil, and the way the cooks jumped as he walked in.

He turned to Amy, pulling on her coat, finished for the day.

'Well, I'm off,' she said. He had the most peculiar expression on his face. 'What are you looking at?' she said.

229

Alain stared hard into her eyes and smiled a wicked proprietorial grin.

'Nothing,' he said. 'See you tomorrow. We can't do it unless you're there, remember.'

She smiled and moved towards him. 'I know,' she said.

He took hold of the lapels of her coat, and pulled her toward him for a kiss.

Amy pushed him playfully away.

'Behave,' she said.

He took the tip of her index finger in his hand, pulled it to his mouth, kissed it and touched his lips.

27

Things had run late at the office again. A last minute
'legal nicety', which was never any such thing, was
holding him up. Miss Cartwright would kill him. Added
to this he didn't have his car. It was in the garage with a
rattle being seen to. His whole life seemed to have a
bloody rattle right at the moment. He dashed down to
reception and talked to George, the commissionaire.

'Has that cab not arrived yet?'

'No, sir,' said George, and looked at him sympa-
thetically. He looked so flustered.

'Can you call them and cancel. I'll hail one,' Jack said.

'Certainly, sir.'

Jack dashed into the street. Where were the cabs
tonight? He stood with one foot in the road. Waving his
arm wildly at any vehicle painted black. A cab came
along with its light on, but the driver waved him aside
and switched it off. Jack looked at his watch.

'Shit,' he said.

He stepped further into the road. Another cab was
coming, he could see it at the lights just up the road. It was
for hire, but in the wrong lane, he'd have to attract its
attention or it'd just flow on past. He tried to indicate to it
by waving wildly. It seemed to be pulling up on the other
side of the road, heading for the register office.

Jack glanced across. A large wedding party was

gathered. Young people mostly, throwing confetti and dressed to the nines. Jack smiled.

Then, suddenly his face froze.

At the centre of all the attention was Amy. She was wearing a hat, a rather stylish thing, at an angle on her blonde hair. On the lapel of her suit, in a spray of white, like pearls, was a corsage of lily of the valley. She was holding a bouquet.

There was a thud in Jack's stomach.

The cab pulled up and stopped.

'Yeah, mate?' said the driver.

'Oh, yeah, yeah,' said Jack, distracted. He got into the back of the cab, giving no destination but staring at the bride on the other side of the street.

'Yeah?'

'Islington . . .' said Jack. 'Islington.'

The cab edged slowly back into the traffic as Jack stared at the wedding party. There was Alain, a red carnation in his button hole. He watched as Alain slipped his arm through Amy's and turned to kiss her. Jack could barely bear to watch. There was Susan, laughing, and wiping a tear from her eye at the same time, as she took their photograph, standing on the steps of the register office.

Suddenly the cab picked up speed and he was being whisked away from it all, through the London traffic. The cab driver looked nervous of him, he was checking him in the mirror, as Jack sat, frozen in the back seat.

He looked as if he was in a state of shock.

On Sunday he went to his parents' town house for lunch. They had a mews house just off Camden Hill Square in Holland Park. Jack had always been a rare visitor, not just because the house had always made him uneasy with its porcelain perfection, and plumped cushion obsession, but because, well, whenever he was there it all invariably ended in a row, at the centre of which he found himself.

Michael opened the door to Jack. Smiling. First he kissed Sarah, in Jack's arms, on the head. Then he kissed Jack on the cheek.

'Welcome!' he said. He led him through to the dining-room with his arm around Jack. Jack felt something like a trophy, won at rugby, or eights, but it was a warm feeling nevertheless.

In the dining-room Margaret and Phil were enjoying a gin and tonic together, and chatting amiably. Jack felt as if he were on another planet.

After lunch they withdrew to the living-room where Phil tried to entertain Sarah. The little girl still seemed so unusually solemn.

It had all gone terribly well. They all seemed to feel sorry for the poor boy who looked so fed up with everything. Margaret had another gin and tonic.

'Have you sent Felicity that cheque yet?' she asked him.

'No.'

'Well you must. It's very embarrassing for me. It's been over a month and I'm playing bridge with her on Thursday.'

'I resent it,' said Jack.

Phil looked up and smiled wickedly.

'If you resent anyone it should be that dreadful American girl for leaving you in the lurch,' said Margaret.

Michael stood up and crossed the room. He hadn't been listening to the conversation. He was, after all, banned from the Nanny Business. He was looking at his granddaughter. He looked worried as he stared at her, flopped listlessly on the floor, uninterested in any distraction that Phil could provide.

'What's wrong with Sarah?' he said.

'I don't know,' said Jack. 'She's been off-colour for a few days.'

Margaret glanced across and looked back at Jack. 'Teething probably.'

'She doesn't talk to me anymore,' said Jack, sadly.

Margaret tutted. 'She's a baby, she doesn't talk to anyone.'

Phil looked at the baby sadly and then turned to face the room. 'She's pining,' she said.

'What for?' said Margaret, almost laughing derisively.

' "That dreadful American Girl".'

'Don't talk such rot, Phil,' said Margaret.

Phil stood up and faced her.

'Shut up, Margaret!' said Michael.

Margaret grabbed the pearls at her neck, shocked. 'Phil!' And in her own house too!

Michael turned towards his son. 'And so's he,' he said.

Margaret rounded on her husband. 'Michael!'

He looked at her coldly for a moment.

'Shut up, Margaret,' he said.

Margaret was so shocked that she was, miraculously, silenced. Michael hadn't dared tell her to shut up since about 1957. She waited for a moment hoping that it was a jest. It was not.

The brief familial bliss had broken down irrevocably.

'I can't be doing with this,' said Jack, picking up Sarah. 'We have to go.'

He took her out of the house, leaving behind him a stunned silence. It was the first time he'd not been the cause of a 'scene' in this house. He was terribly, terribly proud of his father.

He dashed out into the street, he took a gulp of the cool crisp air, and braced himself. Everything was so fucking complicated again. Families were the end. Families: those things enforced upon you by defective genes. He got into his car and strapped Sarah into her baby seat in the back.

There was a tap on the roof.

'Could you give me a lift home?' said Phil.

'I'm not going your way.'

Phil opened the door and got in. 'Thanks,' she said.

Jack sat in the driving seat refusing to start the engine. He laid his head back on the head-rest in despair at it all.

'Why are you so upset?' asked Phil.

He sighed heavily.

'I just wish you'd all leave me alone to get on with my life.'

Phil tapped the back of his hand lightly. 'If we'd done that you'd be drunk in a gutter somewhere and Margaret would have Sarah wearing pearls, and going to dinner parties, and playing bridge by now.'

'You don't understand.'

Phil thought for a moment. The boy was upset. 'Of course I don't,' she said. 'I've only lost my husband and my daughter. How could I?'

Jack had been staring at the steering wheel, furious with them all. Now he looked at Phil.

'I'm sorry,' he said.

'That's all right.'

'I feel so guilty all the time. It's terrible.'

'Of course you do. We all do. Every time one of us picks Sarah up and feels happy, we feel it.'

'It's awful . . . '

There was a pause as they stared out of the front of the car onto the cold London streets.

'Dear, dear Sarah has gone and there's nothing we can do about that,' said Phil. 'You mustn't feel guilty, Jack. That would be a waste of two lives . . . three lives. You can't have Sarah grow up and saying her childhood was fine; lots of nice nannies, but my father never really got over the death of my mother.'

Jack loved Phil so much, he couldn't speak. She touched the back of his hand again.

'And she won't have to . . . or wouldn't've if you hadn't screwed it up.'

Jack was unsure, at first, of what she meant. What had he screwed up, in the whole course of this, of all the many things he'd screwed up?

He stared hard into her face for guidance.

'She was lovely, Jack. Silly boy . . . drive me home.'

Jack's car pulled up outside Phil's first-floor flat in Ladbroke Grove, a white-painted place, with crumbling pillars at the door. Shrubs out front. He stared at them for a moment.

'I saw Amy yesterday,' he said.

'Oh yes, how was she?'

'She was getting married,' he said.

He wished, in some ways, he'd not told her this. At least she had some hope for him, even if it was only for today.

'I see,' said Phil. 'Come in for some tea?'

'I won't.'

'Please?' said Phil, and she seemed to need him to.

'OK.'

They got out of the car. Jack walked up to the pathway, but Phil hung behind a little.

'I've run out of milk,' she said, typically. 'I'll just get some from the shop.'

'I'll go,' he said.

'No. You take Sarah in. I'll only be five minutes. Put the kettle on.'

It had been a while, as well, since he'd been to Phil's place. It hadn't changed. It hadn't actually changed since about 1968. Still in pride of place on a writing table were the photographs of Phil when she was a revolutionary in the sixties. One of her posing rather primly with Bertrand Russell, and a more recent one, twenty years between them, but the same pose with Bruce Kent. A CND poster, one of the originals, in a Habitat frame above the mantelpiece. The place felt cold, as if she didn't have much to live on. You couldn't see the carpet, the entire floor was made up of rugs. Books everywhere. Brass Indian vases. Heavy lumps of mud-like African sculpture. You couldn't break anything in this room if you brought a young bull into it. It was rather welcoming. It smelt of things. Things other than air freshener and polish, unlike his own mother's house.

He went into the kitchen to boil the kettle. Phil still had one of those old thin metal things with a spout that whistled. The gas jet needed lighting. He reached for a book of matches laying on the draining board. As he struck the match, he read the flap of the book. 117 Brasserie. A dart of recognition hit him. That was the place where Amy worked, wasn't it? He filled the kettle and put it on to the jet.

There was the sound of light young feet trotting down the stairs from above.

237

He looked toward the living-room door, through the beaded curtains.

'Phil! You're back early. What happened?' said a voice, young, female, and American.

Jack looked towards the as yet unopened door.

'Amy . . . ?'

Amy burst into the room.

It seemed almost impossible. It was impossible. What was going on? Jack's mind was racing. Was he hallucinating? It was possible, he told himself, after all he'd been through, that he'd finally gone mad. That he was welding together all the elements of his life into one first-floor flat in Ladbroke Grove.

'Jack. . . ! Sarah!' said Amy, with a look of equal shock on her face.

Jack shook his head from side to side. If this were a dream, then it would be unfair. If this were real, it was incredible.

'What're you doing here?' he said, lamely. 'Where's Alain?'

Amy twitched and giggled.

'With his wife, I hope.'

'His wife?' said Jack, slowly.

'Alain and Susan got hitched yesterday.'

'But . . . ' There seemed no more to say. Jack was mentally pinching himself. He walked to the window and stared out. Phil had been working behind the scenes here, he realised. She'd taken Amy in as a lodger expressly to spring this kind of trap. She was a clever woman. It was the greatest gift of a former mother-in-law. It was a genuine desire for peace.

Amy ran over to where Sarah was pulling at the threads of an old battered rug. She picked her up and walked with

238

her towards the window where the little girl wanted to pull at the strands of the lace curtains.

'I missed you,' said Amy.

He turned to look at her, at her fresh, lovely, beautiful face. She was staring out into the street.

'I missed you too,' said Jack.

'I wasn't talking to you,' she replied. 'But I'm touched, nevertheless.'

Jack coughed. 'Well, that is, we . . . we missed you . . . both of us.' He couldn't cover any more. 'We want you back.'

She turned around, the light of the street behind her, falling on her arms.

'My rates have gone up. You can't afford me.'

Jack shuffled on the rugs. Sarah was staring up at her, bright-eyed, and full of life again.

'Not as a nanny,' he said

She took her eyes away from Sarah and concentrated on his. His heart was pounding. She enjoyed, for a moment, the rare consideration of such a prospect.

'In that case you certainly can't afford me.'

'Is that a yes?'

She swivelled on the rugs, delighting Sarah.

'It's a maybe.'

'That'll do,' said Jack.

She narrowed her eyes.

'There's one condition.'

'Name it.'

'I get to tell your mother.'

Epilogue

It was a beautiful Saturday afternoon, in midsummer, and everyone looked magnificent. Jack especially so, with a wildly extravagant waistcoat he'd had made. He'd dressed his office window, across the street from the register office, with flowers too. Anna had even helped him arrange them.

They had stepped out into sunshine, Amy and Jack, spilling out on to the street in what Jack considered to be a much more joyous display than any he'd ever witnessed from his desk during idle afternoons gazing out.

Everyone was clicking with their cameras, and dipping into little cardboard cartons of confetti. Horseshoes and bells and knots stamped out of paper fluttered around them like butterflies. There was hysterical laughter from all, and everyone seemed to be kissing and hugging each other.

There was Pamela with a corsage of lilies on her lapel, up from Cambridge especially, with her handsome young boyfriend on her arm, clicking away with an Olympus. They had that silly look on their faces that young people have at weddings which says, 'next time it might be us'.

Amy, in her flowing dress, with Sarah in her arms, turned to kiss Jack on the steps. As they finally pulled their mouths apart, Jack glanced across at Phil, wiping a tear from her eye. She was wearing the largest floppy felt hat he'd ever seen.

He thought back over the last year and a half. He could barely believe that it had been this long already. He glanced at William, nipping in and out of the guests with his little Kodak fun camera, bright and smart and charming. It seemed incredible now that they'd spent so many nights together sleeping in the pile of leaves behind the gardener's green slatted hut in the square. He watched as William moved the official photographer out of the way, as he set up his tripod trying hopelessly to get The Standard Group Shot, so that he could snap away with his little cardboard box of a camera.

It was good to see Susan too, laughing and joking, as she made outrageous advances to Rob. Jack was relieved that Alain had obviously decided to stay at home today. Still it would be fun to bowl into his brasserie one day with Amy and order the entire menu.

He looked at Sarah, giggling in Amy's arms. Everyone seemed to want to kiss her on the head. Attention that she obviously adored. She had hair now, of course, and was the prettiest little girl in the world. She'd also become what Jack lovingly described as a flirt. She had a particular way of gaining attention from all. She was very like him, and he knew that.

There was a deep feeling in his stomach, deep swathes of genuine happiness. My God, it was a good feeling. An incredible feeling, one that he'd never expected ever to feel again. But he had. And he'd learned not to feel guilty about it. Thank God he'd not descended into the mire that he was capable of. If Sarah were here, he knew what she'd say. She would have been furious with him for going to pieces, for almost abandoning their daughter. She'd be proud of him for finding Amy, he knew that, because Amy loved Sarah so naturally, like she would have done.

He looked at his father as he circulated among the guests, shaking their hands and joking. Jack watched him for a while, smiling broadly. He remembered the time his father had turned up at the new house, when he was taking slugs of Scotch. He hadn't realised then, of course, that it had been his father's plan all along, to lay Sarah on his bed. It had saved his life. It was a miracle that he'd trusted him so much, enough to have stood his ground, and flown in the face of Margaret and Phil.

It was, he supposed, his father that he had to thank for the gift of his daughter. He was a wiser man than he knew. He didn't just listen, he acted as well. Jack was so glad that the frost had thawed between them. But for this, it never would have done. He looked again at Sarah, happy in Amy's arms. She was so like him, he wondered how much he was like his father too. They both had battles with themselves.

His father turned and looked across at him, as he stood there. He smiled and winked at him. It was an astonishing gesture of affection. A gesture that had, until now, been impossible between them.

Then he caught sight of his mother. Her arms rigid by her side, resolutely refusing to speak to Michael or anyone else. She was dressed in black, of all things. Oh God, he thought, and walked over.

'Well?' he said, happily, trying to lighten her spirits, wanting to catch her and somehow convey the love that he felt for her too.

'Well . . .' said Margaret with a troubled sigh.

'Well, come on, spit it out, Mother.'

'What?'

'Whatever's sticking in your throat?'

'Well it's . . . I'm still quite speechless, that's all.'

Michael stepped in. 'Some good will come of every-thing . . .' he said, with a smirk on his face, looking happily at Jack again.

'Michael!' said Margaret, biting at her lip and adjusting her hat.

'Oh come on, can't you simply say you think it's marvellous?' Jack said to cajole her. 'Say it's wonderful, all the things you're supposed to say?'

'Oh, I do, I do,' said Margaret, unconvincingly, 'I mean, I really do.' She looked as if she was about to burst into tears, or take a swipe at a passing tourist. 'Of course I do. It would be churlish . . . I mean, honestly. I do.'

'Good,' said Jack, acknowledging her weak attempt as the best she could do.

'It'll just take a bit of getting used to, that's all. I really am very happy, darling. Really.'

She looked at Michael, who looked as disbelieving as his son.

'Really . . .' she said.

The photographer, a little man in a shiny suit that had seen a lot of weddings, walked in to control the throng.

'Can we have the bride and groom, please? The bride and groom.'

William tucked his fun camera into his pocket.

They walked to the top of the stairs to pose, everyone clapping, and stood between the Doric columns of the civic building. Designed for just such perfect shots as this. They smiled, smiles that could barely believe what they'd actually just done. At last this public commitment, in front of everyone, a confirmed commitment that was real, so real that there was no doubt it would be lasting.

Slightly embarrassed by all the fuss, the happy couple held hands and posed for the cameras of their friends.

Jack raised his camera to his eye.

'Give her a kiss for God's sake!' he shouted.

William looked at him nervously for a moment, but held his ground on the step of the register office and kissed his bride. A tear fell down Phil's cheek as she kissed her new husband back.

Their guests cheered. Jack turned to Amy, holding Sarah, and kissed her on the lips.

William called Jack and Amy and Sarah up on to the steps for a photograph.

All the cameras clicked. There was no doubt in anyone's minds who would be next.

Coming soon from Mandarin Paperbacks

KERRI BROOKS

French Kiss

A GLORIOUSLY FUNNY NEW ROMANTIC COMEDY FROM
THE MAKERS OF *FOUR WEDDINGS AND A FUNERAL*
STARRING MEG RYAN AND KEVIN KLINE

Kate thinks her life is pretty near perfect. She is engaged
to Charlie, a doctor, and she's emigrating to Canada, a
country she infinitely prefers to her native USA. Canada
is ordered, safe, straightforward – everything she values.

But things start to go wrong when Charlie doesn't come
back from his Paris convention, preferring to stay with
the *femme fatale* he meets there. Getting on a plane to
fetch him back, Kate finds herself sitting next to an
unshaven, garrulous, distinctly shady Frenchman called
Luc. And things go from bad to worse when she can't get
rid of Luc, or get hold of Charlie, or find her luggage once
she's in the city of romance . . .

Polygram Filmed Entertainment presents a Working Title Production in
association with Prufrock Pictures. A Lawrence Kasdan Film. Meg Ryan,
Kevin Kline, Timothy Hutton, Jean Reno, Suzanne Anbeh, Francois
Cluzet. Written by Adam Brooks. Produced by Tim Bevan, Eric Fellner,
Meg Ryan, Kathryn F. Galan. Directed by Lawrence Kasdan.

Also available from Mandarin Paperbacks

THOMAS HARRIS

The Silence of the Lambs

THE MOST FRIGHTENING BOOK YOU'LL EVER READ

There's a killer on the loose who knows that beauty is only skin deep, and a trainee investigator who's trying to save her own hide.

The only man that can help is locked in an asylum. But he's willing to put a brave face on – if it will help him escape.

'Thrillers don't come any better than this . . . razor sharp entertainment, beautifully constructed and brilliantly written. It takes us to places in the mind where few writers have the talent or sheer nerve to venture'
Clive Barker

'The best book I've read for a very long time . . . subtle, horrific and splendid'
Roald Dahl

AMY TAN

The Joy Luck Club

'A brilliant first novel, *The Joy Luck Club* is the story of four mothers and their first-generation Chinese-American daughters; two generations of women struggling to come to terms with their cultural identity. Tan writes from the heart, cutting sharp edges with wit, wisdom and a gentle and delicate precision. Completely compelling'

Time Out

'Honest, moving and beautifully courageous'
Alice Walker

'She is both a consummate storyteller and a writer whose prose manages to be emotionally charged without a trace of sentimentality'

Sunday Times

'Pure enchantment'

Mail On Sunday

A List of Film and TV Tie-In Titles
Available from Mandarin

While every effort is made to keep prices low, it is sometimes necessary to increase prices at short notice. Mandarin Paperbacks reserves the right to show new retail prices on covers which may differ from those previously advertised in the text or elsewhere.

The prices shown below were correct at the time of going to press.

All these books are available at your bookshop or newsagent, or can be ordered direct from the address below. Just tick the titles you want and fill in the form below.

Cash Sales Department, PO Box 5, Rushden, Northants NN10 6YX.
Fax: 01933 414047 : Phone: 01933 414000.

Please send cheque, payable to 'Reed Book Services Ltd.', or postal order for purchase price quoted and allow the following for postage and packing:

£1.00 for the first book, 50p for the second; **FREE POSTAGE AND PACKING FOR THREE BOOKS OR MORE PER ORDER.**

NAME (Block letters) ....

ADDRESS ....

....

☐ I enclose my remittance for ....

☐ I wish to pay by Access/Visa Card Number

Expiry Date

Signature ....

Please quote our reference: MAND